Fic Fic Bro
Brown, Carolyn.

To trust

TO TRUST

A Broken Roads Romance

Other books by Carolyn Brown

Love Is
A Falling Star
All the Way from Texas
The Yard Rose
The Ivy Tree
Lily's White Lace
That Way Again
The Wager
Trouble in Paradise
The PMS Club

The *Drifters and Dreamers Romance* Series:

Morning Glory
Sweet Tilly
Evening Star

The *Love's Valley Historical Romance* Series:

Redemption
Choices
Absolution
Chances
Promises

The *Promised Land Romance* Series:

Willow
Velvet
Gypsy
Garnet
Augusta

The *Land Rush Romance* Series:

Emma's Folly
Violet's Wish
Maggie's Mistake
Just Grace

TO TRUST

•

Carolyn Brown

AVALON BOOKS
NEW YORK

Published by Thomas Bouregy & Co., Inc.
160 Madison Avenue, New York, NY 10016

Library of Congress Cataloging-in-Publication Data

Brown, Carolyn, 1948–
    To trust / Carolyn Brown.
        p. cm.
    ISBN 978-0-8034-9874-7 (acid-free paper)
    1. Divorced women—Fiction. 2. Oklahoma—Fiction.
3. Domestic fiction. I. Title.
    PS3552.R685275T6 2008
    813'.54—dc22

                                        2007027167

PRINTED IN THE UNITED STATES OF AMERICA
ON ACID-FREE PAPER
BY HADDON CRAFTSMEN, BLOOMSBURG, PENNSYLVANIA

This one is for Bobby Rucker.

Chapter One

Dee Hooper was bone-tired from the fourteen-hundred-mile drive, and the worst was yet to come. The devastation of her heart was nothing compared to what waited less than a mile away. In spite of the blistering Oklahoma heat, cold dread filled her as she turned into the driveway. The swinging wrought-iron sign above the entrance announced that she'd just turned onto Roxie's property. "Roxie's B&B," it advertised. Most folks had known it as Roxie's Bed and Breakfast for close to fifty years. Roxie referred to it as Roxie's Blessin's and Bellyachin'. Dee hoped today was the blessin's.

Dee stomped on the brakes of the big, black dual-cab Silverado pickup. "Good God! Roxie painted the place red!" She stared ahead at the two-story house now Crayola-red with white trim. Finally, she eased the

1

truck into the multicarport to the south of the main house. There was Roxie's old '86 white Cadillac, not a fleck of dust or a bird dropping anywhere on it.

A southern woman's social dignity is determined by the way she keeps her Caddy clean. Just one of Roxie's many adages. A newer, purple Ford Escort and an older-model black Buick were parked on either side of the Cadillac. Both were dusty, looking downright shabby next to the old Caddy. Evidently, Roxie had guests this weekend.

Dee checked her reflection in the rearview mirror, reapplied lipstick, and brushed her short, light-brown hair back, but she couldn't erase the bags under her light-green eyes or the sadness in her face. Her hands trembled, her breath caught in her chest, and her feet felt like they were made of lead, but there was nothing to do but go face the music. The white indentation on the ring finger of her left hand would take a while to vanish, but the scars on her soul would probably last forever.

"Time to go get a dose of 'I told you so,' but a southern lady keeps a smile on her face and her head held high whether she's wading in tall cotton or deep manure," she whispered, another of Roxie's proverbs.

She took a deep breath and stepped out of the air-conditioned truck. A blast of still, hot, dry air tried to suffocate her. Not a breeze between her and the Gulf of Mexico. The July heat bore down on her like an anvil. It scorched her lungs and sucked every drop of moisture from her body. She crossed the plush green grass, wondering how much water Roxie used every day to keep the lawn alive, and opened the front door without knocking. "Hello," she called out. Nothing but silence answered her.

Not one thing had changed. The top of the foyer table was so shiny, she could use it for a mirror. The wood floors looked like they had a layer of glass on them. She could see the reflection of her khaki walking shorts and flashes of the red in her T-shirt as she walked across the floor. She meandered through the dining room and kitchen, and peeked out the back-door window. There was Roxie with several other people, sitting on the wooden lawn chairs, sipping something cold-looking from tall, frosty glasses. It had to be tea or lemonade.

Dee opened the door, inhaled deeply, and went to face them.

"Well, I do declare, just look what the dogs have dragged up and the cats wouldn't have." Roxie pushed her sunglasses down on the tip of her nose and peered out over the top. "Did you finally come to your senses, girl? Don't just stand there. You'll die of a heat stroke. Pour yourself a glass of tea and find a cool spot under the shade tree. It's too hot to breathe. Now sit down and tell me that you got rid of that rich man."

"Dee?" Jack Brewer said right behind her.

She'd been so intent on seeing her grandmother, Roxie, she hadn't even looked at the other people in the group. "Jack?"

Her childhood fishing buddy, the proverbial boy next

door, and her best friend all those years ago, had changed in seven years. His face was a study in angles seven years before. Now it had filled out somewhat and looked good on him. He'd been a tall, gangly kid from the time they were in kindergarten, but now his T-shirt stretched to cover muscles in his chest and arms. And where did those yellow flecks in his hazel eyes come from? Surely it was a contact-lens trick, because he'd worn thick glasses from the time he was in first grade. Where an eighteen-year-old boy had stood, a man had taken his place.

"I just came over for a glass of tea. Hotter'n hell on the judgment day, ain't it? I'll get on back across the yard and leave you ladies, now. You'll have a lot of catching up to do." He turned his back and walked across the yard to his own place right next door.

"Come anytime, Jack. You know we always like the company," Roxie said. "Now, girl, you sit over there but only if you've got rid of that man you took up with. If he's out there in whatever you drove, then you remember what I said. It still stands. You got a home here any time you want it, but that man's not to darken my doorway."

"I know Roxie. He's gone. But I got to admit. I didn't get rid of him. He got rid of me. But gone is gone, isn't it?"

"Yes, ma'am, it is. Divorced yet?" Roxie pushed her glasses back up on her nose and readjusted her broad-brimmed straw hat with a wide, red satin band around the crown.

"Yes, he and his family pulled some kind of strings.

It's been annulled. After seven years they got it annulled. Funny, ain't it? But they wanted the new wife and the baby to be solid in the church. Seven years and it never happened," Dee said.

"Well, God won't lay that one to your charge. Not for that lapse of good common sense," Roxie said. "You bring any baggage with you?"

"Just what's out there in my truck. Back end is loaded with my personal things. That's all. No kids. He didn't want kids. At least that's what he said all these years. Came right down to it, he didn't want them with me. The old girlfriend from high school was a different matter when she came home from France." Dee sat down on the last remaining wooden lounge chair, the back of her legs sticking to the oak before she'd even gotten comfortable.

She looked closer at the woman on her left. "Mimosa! Is that you?"

"Yes, darling, it's your dear mother." Mimosa smiled. "Come here and give your Momma a hug. It'll slide all your makeup off, but Lord, girl, we ain't seen each other in a long time."

Dee hugged her mother tightly and then stooped to hug Roxie.

"You are my Aunt Dee?" The young girl on her right asked.

"Bodine?" Dee could scarcely believe her eyes. The precocious four-year-old had grown up. "What is that you are wearing?"

"Today I am a southern princess drinking mint juleps

in the heat of the day," she announced with a wave of her hand. She wore a pink headband with a pouf of net and a big, yellow plastic sunflower held on with a twist-tie from a bread wrapper. She had pushed a bright red satin dress, with black lace trim around the neck and hem, up to her waist showing her bathing suit bottom underneath it. Freckles had been tossed randomly across her pert little turned-up nose. Her crystal-blue eyes were exactly like her mother's. Her kinky light-brown hair was pulled back into a ponytail.

"Found a bunch of Halloween costumes on sale after the holiday last fall. Bodine can be anyone she pleases. Sometimes she's a princess. Sometimes she's a pirate," Roxie said. "Gives her character and teaches her individuality."

"Where's Tally?" Dee asked after her sister.

"She's got another month in county for hot checks and then she'll be home," Mimosa said.

"Good Lord!" Dee exclaimed.

Roxie shook her finger at Dee. "Don't you be taking on that tone. You married a dang fool and spent seven years up there in that gawdforsaken place without ever coming home to see me. She just got a year in county lock-up for those hot checks, and I get to see her every weekend."

"Roxie, you told me when I left not to come back unless I got rid of him," Dee reminded her, amazed that she'd just walked back into her dysfunctional family's life like she'd only been gone thirty minutes on a trip to the store.

"And I meant it, but you could have left him sooner," Roxie said.

Bodine waved her hand dramatically. "I declare it's an abominable sin to waste our precious breath arguing in this kind of heat. Here, Aunt Dee, I'll pour you a glass of tea. Lemon? We'll talk about nice things. I'm reading *Gone with the Wind*. What are you reading?"

"You're only eleven years old and reading something like that? And yes, lemon would be nice, thank you." Dee still couldn't believe her niece wasn't four and talking with a lisp.

"Yes, ma'am, I am eleven years old." Bodine nodded regally so her headpiece wouldn't fall off. "But you taught me to read before you left with that man who started the war of northern aggression. I'm glad you finally shot him through the heart and buried him under the compost pile. That's the only place fitting to bury a Yankee, you know. Just put him out there with the rest of the . . ." She stopped dead and twisted her mouth to one side. ". . . manure," she finished.

"Bodine!" Dee chided.

"Leave her alone," Mimosa said. "She's right. But we're glad to have the prodigal daughter back home."

"You're one to talk about prodigal daughters. What happened to the last truck driver?" Dee asked.

"He retired and so did I. I've come home to take care of my dear Roxie," Mimosa said.

"Hmmph," Roxie snorted. "I've heard that story so many times I know the words by heart. Besides, I'll be taking care of the whole ragtag lot of you until I'm a hundred years old. I'll drop dead right after I take a pecan pie out of the oven, and you'll all be pushing up daisies long before me. The rules are still the same. I'll abide a lot, but I don't cotton to men slapping women no matter what the cause."

Dee nodded.

"That's my girl," Roxie said. "Now, enough of this heat. We've got air-conditioning in the house. It's time to start supper, and then we'll all help Dee get her stuff put back in her room. And, honey, it is right good to have you back home. Tally will be glad to know her sister is here when she gets out of county next month."

Dee trailed behind them, bringing in the tray with the pitcher and glasses. After all, the prodigal must do extensive penance for committing the two unforgivable sins. Number one: marrying a Yankee. Number two: leaving southern Oklahoma to live in that *gawdforsaken* place. It would take a lot of tray-toting to redeem her. Even on the judgment day, she might be assigned extra atonement for the first twenty thousand years of eternity.

Roxie hung her straw hat on the nail beside the back door and started giving orders like a drill sergeant. "Bodine, you make us another pitcher of tea and slice the lemons. Thin, now, you hear? Mimosa, you can make the biscuits and cut up the okra. I'll fry the chicken. If you haven't forgotten how, Dee, you can make the fresh pickles and slice the tomatoes. Eggs are in the refrigerator, already boiled. Dee, you can devil them. Southern style. Don't you be puttin' nothing in the eggs that you learned up there among those heathens."

Roxie fluffed up her hair, the same brilliant red she'd always had. Right out of the Clairol box. She'd been born with red hair and she swore she'd be laid out in her coffin with the same color. She wore electric-blue Spandex capri pants with a bright red tank top, covered with an oversized shirt of some kind of gauzy material that looked like it had been constructed of a Confederate flag. Dee had never seen her without her pearl earrings. She even slept in them just in case she was wrong about living to be a hundred and still making pecan pies. She wouldn't think of facing off with St. Peter without her pearl earrings. Dee had also never seen her grandmother in anything but high-heeled shoes. She gardened in them, cooked in them, and went to church every Sunday morning in them. Only difference was, the ones she gardened in weren't made of Italian leather.

"Why didn't you just bail Tally out of those hot checks?" Dee peeled cucumbers and sliced them wafer-thin, along with onions, into brine made of salt and cold water.

"I told her after the first two times that if she did it again, she was steppin' up to the plate and takin' her castor oil. I don't make promises I don't intend to deliver. Judge over there at the courthouse asked me if I wanted to pay the fines for the checks again. I told him that she could do her year in county and maybe she'd learn a lesson. Just like I meant it when you left here with that sissified, pretty city boy. You wasn't comin' home until you got rid of him."

"Was he really pretty?" Bodine asked.

"Yes, he was very pretty," Dee answered.

Roxie deftly cut up the chicken, rolled it in a flour mixture that contained her own herbs and spices, and made the Colonel's take a back seat. "I never thought he was pretty. That diamond earring glitterin' in his ear was pretty. Guess it's all in the eye of the beholder."

Mimosa started to say something but shut her mouth with a heavy sigh. Dee noticed that her mother hadn't progressed past the hippie stage where she'd gotten stuck back before Dee and Tally had been born and shifted over to Roxie to raise. Back when Mimosa changed truck driver husbands as often as she changed her hair color. She still wore bell-bottom jeans, floral shirts with flowing sleeves, platform shoes, and pale pink lipstick. At least her dark-brown hair was short now instead of long and straight as a board. That was most likely because it took only one box of dye to keep it colored when it was short.

"Soon as supper is over, we'll get that truck unloaded and your things toted up to your room." Roxie dropped the chicken in hot grease, let it brown rapidly on one side, then turned it over and put a lid on the cast-iron skillet.

"You didn't make my room into a B&B room?" Dee asked.

"Retired two years ago from that. Got to be more bellyachin' than blessin', so me and Bodine, she was the only one here at the time, we had us a regular executive meeting and decided we was tired of the gig. We only got one huntin' bunch we still let use the place, and I'm thinkin' on letting Molly Branson have that business this fall. She's about ready to throw in the dishrag too. Fightin' with cancer. Three of us, me and Molly and Etta, we're all ready for retirement," Roxie said.

"I'm so sorry about Molly. I'll have to go see her soon. So my room is still the same?"

"Same as the day you left it. I figured sooner or later you'd see through all Ray's citified ways and come home." Roxie gave her a brief hug when she passed from one side of the kitchen to the other.

"The earring and ponytail disappeared pretty fast when we got to Pennsylvania. His father saw to that when he made him vice president of that big company they own." Dee was amazed that she could talk about Ray without wanting to cry. Even more amazed that she was taking up for him.

"If he did you dirty, why are you defending him?" Mimosa asked. "I can't remember defending a one of my husbands who treated me shabbily."

"I'm not taking up for him. I'm just trying to explain. Maybe it's because if I don't, then I feel like a bigger fool than I was. I'm so mad I could chew up oak trees and spit out toothpicks. I almost, and I said *almost*, shoved the settlement back into his father's face. But I didn't. I figured it was payment for seven years of being stupid. Every time I withdraw a check from the bank on that account, I'll remember it and not make the same mistake again."

"Now, that's my girl." Roxie nodded seriously. "You

hear that? She's got her head on just like a Hooper woman. She'll do just fine. Don't be lettin' them pickles set too long now in the brine. They'll get soft for sure. Just a few minutes, then put them in half vinegar, half ice water."

"Yes, ma'am, and Mimosa, don't you dare burn that okra. I haven't had a bite of fried okra in seven years." Dee managed a weak smile.

"It's a wonder you're still alive!" Bodine exclaimed dramatically.

Mimosa threw an arm around Dee as she reached for a bowl. "Malnourished, I'm sure. I swear I can feel your bones sticking out, but then you never did have enough meat on your body. Wait until Sunday when we all go see Tally. Now that girl has got just plumb buffed up in that jail. Lifting weights and all."

"I can't wait," Dee lied sweetly. She'd expected a bigger dressing-down than what she'd gotten, so she shouldn't bear ill will toward going to the county jail to see her older sister, Bodine's mother. She'd only have to go four times, if Tally was indeed getting out in a month. Carrying the tea tray. Visiting her sister in jail. Small prices for the error of her ways.

"We'll go right after church," Roxie said. "You did bring gloves and hats in that big old horse of a truck, didn't you?"

"Roxie, gloves and hats went out of style years ago." Dee drained the brine from the pickles and slid them into the vinegar solution. Then she began peeling eggs.

"Honey, styles may come and styles may go, but a

southern woman does not grace the inside of the Lord's house without the proper attire. That includes gloves and a hat. Now if you didn't bring them, I can loan you some of mine. There's a new trend on right now having to do with some red hat club they've gotten up. All over that poem I've liked for years about wearing purple when I am old. I was down in Ardmore just last week, in that Cato's store and lo and behold there was hats. I bought six. So you can take your pick. There's a gorgeous red one with a big black bow at the back," Roxie said.

"I do have a good black dress," Dee said. "But I don't have black gloves, so I'll just have to wear the dress without gloves and a hat. You know what the rule is about wearing black gloves in the summertime. White after Easter. Black after Labor Day."

"I've got a drawer full of white gloves. Any length you want, sugar," Mimosa told her.

"And I'm wearing a straw hat with a green bow and a big, fluffy green dress with no sleeves and lace gloves," Bodine said. "I'll be Scarlett at the Twelve Oaks' barbecue. Only if those silly Baker twins try to talk to me, I'm going to slap them so hard they'll have a red face for a week."

"Bodine!" Mimosa's tone left no room for discussion.

"Okay, okay. I'll try to be a lady. Is that better?" Bodine asked.

"Much. I do swear, Tally's attitude rubs off on you entirely too much, young lady. It's a good thing I arrived when I did or else you'd be nothing but a common hoyden. Now let's get supper over with so we can take a glass of cold lemonade to the back porch and catch a breath of fresh air while the sun sets. It's my favorite time of the day, since I've retired," Mimosa said.

Dee didn't think she could eat a single bite of the supper, but she managed to clean up two plates of pure cholesterol. Her fat cells squirmed in ecstasy. Her muscles dreaded the run the next morning to work off all those extra fat grams and calories. And then, to top it all off, she accepted a lemonade to carry to the porch to watch the sun set.

"Ah." Roxie sipped the icy cold sweet drink. It was her favorite time of the day too. A time when she could remember Henry and the good times. Back before the whole world went to the devil in a handbasket and her family turned into a bunch of ragtags that she could barely keep together.

"Wonderful." Dee nodded in agreement.

"Southern women never drink." Bodine sipped her lemonade.

"No, sugar, they don't. They sip. And sip. And sip." Mimosa giggled.

"That's what Roxie says too," Bodine giggled with her grandmother. "And you know what else she says? She says that I have to listen to Tally, because she's my mother. That I have to listen to you because you're my grandmother. And what y'all say is important, but what she says is the law and it's the most important thing in the world. She says that what she says goes right over the top of what anyone else says because she's the grand matri . . . matri . . . queen of the whole family."

"And don't you ever forget it," Dee told her seriously.

"Evenin', ladies," Jack called from halfway across the lawn. "Mind if I join you for a bit of conversation that doesn't have to do with the price of a loaf of bread?"

"Come on around, Jack. Got a rocking chair special waiting with your name on it. How's business this evening?" Roxie said.

His smile would bring toothpaste commercials to their knees. Dee's breath caught in her chest.

Good Lord, Almighty, she argued with her fluttering heart. *This is Jack Brewer, the computer geek from next door who had no ambition except to understand the difference in hard drives. Besides, I'm one month out of a disastrous relationship and I'll never trust another man as long as I live. Not even Jack from next door. Not even if he does look like James Dean.*

"Business has been good today," he answered Roxie's question.

Mimosa held up the remainder of her drink. "Can I get you a lemonade? I'm refilling mine."

He held up a quart jar. "Brought my own iced tea. Sold three gallons of milk, a truckload of soft drinks, a dozen loaves of bread, and enough junk food to keep the weight doctors happy for years."

"I'm surprised you keep the store open," Mimosa said.

"Got to. It's a front and a laundromat for all my mafia money." Jack stole a glance at Dee. She'd changed, not so much anyone else could see, but there was sadness in her eyes.

"Oh, Jack, you're being silly," Bodine giggled. "You're not in the mafia."

"A southern man never tells all his secrets," Jack drawled.

"That would be 'A southern woman never tells all her secrets,'" Bodine told him.

"Well, where did you think southern women learned to keep a secret? We taught them, that's how." Jack let his peripheral vision drink in the sight of Dee's legs. Even if she wasn't tall, she'd always had the most gorgeous legs. It wasn't easy sitting there with her close enough to reach out and touch, but he'd survive. After all, he'd done so forever.

"So you home for good?" he asked.

"I suppose I am." She sipped her drink and looked at him through the pale yellow liquid.

"Want to go fishing tomorrow evening after I shut up shop?" he asked.

She ran the sweating glass across her forehead. "Haven't been fishing in seven years. That would be the night you told me I was making a big mistake going off with Ray. Guess you and Roxie were right. I'd forgotten how hot Oklahoma is in July. I'd love to go fishing. Roxie, we still got rods out in the garage?"

"Sure we do. Just because you ran off doesn't mean the rest of us don't like a mess of fresh catfish ever' so often. I got things to do tomorrow, so I can't go," Roxie said.

"Sorry about that," Jack said.

"I can go," Bodine piped up.

"No, ma'am, you cannot," Roxie said. "Me and you are going to work out in the flower beds tomorrow. There's more weeds than flowers. And Mimosa, you're going to help us too."

"Yes, ma'am." Mimosa narrowed her eyes. She didn't know why Roxie was sending Jack and Dee off together. Sure looked like a case of matchmaking at the wrong time to her, but she wasn't saying a word. After all, Roxie knew Mimosa's daughter far better than she did.

"Good, then come on over to the shop after supper and we'll run down to Buckhorn and see what's biting. You up for fryin' the fish the next day if we catch something?" he asked Roxie.

"I'm always up for a fish fry."

Jack stood up. "Come on and walk me back across the lawn."

"Like when we were little kids, huh?"

"Guess so," Jack said.

When they were on the store's porch, she leaned against the post. "Jack, I'm sorry about that night. You were right, and I was wrong."

"Apology accepted. Good night, Dee," he said as he closed the door.

She heard the lock as it slid home and his footsteps as he checked everything in the store before he left by the back door to go out to his trailer house. For a long time, she leaned against the post. Crickets and frogs combined their singing ability to put on an opera for her. Stars twinkled in the sky but not as much as the fireflies across the two connecting lawns. Bodine giggled. Mimosa said something to Roxie. Dee couldn't understand the words, but the warmth of the tone told her all was well.

Dee was home.

Chapter Two

Jack pulled the tabs on two cans of icy-cold Coke and handed one to Dee. She rolled the cold, sweaty can over her forehead and cheeks before tilting it back and guzzling half the contents.

"Roxie says that ladies sip," Jack reminded her with a chuckle.

"This woman is thirsty, and she's gulping." She came up for air with only the slightest burp.

She wore a pair of cutoff jean shorts and an orange tank top, sandals, and a thick coating of spray-on mosquito repellent over the bare parts of her body. Holding the rod loosely, she watched the red-and-white bobble dance on top of the water. She had been so busy trying to make her life perfect that she hadn't realized how much she'd missed the way she'd been raised.

His jean shorts were frayed at the bottom. His tank top faded to a nondescript shade of gray. His sneakers had no laces and had been white at one time. They sat on their lucky fishing quilt, which hadn't been out of the closet since the night she left to elope with Ray, but she wasn't aware that Jack had put it into storage. She only knew that for the first time in years, she was just Dee Hooper, the girl from Buckhorn Corner, not Dee Suddeth, the woman trying to change her entire life to be a socialite for her husband.

"So I want to know about the last month," he said.

"Why the last month? What about the last seven years?" she asked.

"I know about the last seven years, Dee. Your weekly letter came on Thursday. Roxie, Bodine, and I sat on the porch in good weather, in the kitchen when it wasn't so good, and Roxie read it out loud to us," Jack said in a deep, lazy drawl.

"She never answered a one of those letters, but I had to write. I sure didn't mean for them to become public property," Dee said testily.

"She didn't put them in the newspaper. She only read them to me and Bodine," he reminded her, a bit of edge to his voice. "She loves you. Without Roxie, I wouldn't have stayed, you know?"

"Jack, I'm sorry about your grandparents. I sent flowers and I should have called, but . . ." She let the sentence trail off.

"I know, Dee. I'm sure your husband wouldn't have liked that," Jack said.

"It wasn't Ray. He wouldn't have even known. It was me. I didn't know what to say to you. You were my best friend. If I'd called, I would have unloaded on you and you didn't need that when you were busy grieving for your Poppa and Nanna," she said.

"So the last month?" he asked again. "Remember, I was your best friend, and I want to know." He reached over and pushed the button on the portable CD player. Floyd Cramer's tinkling country piano filled the air.

"Okay, okay. Give me a minute to keep from crying and get my anger worked up."

He waited.

She remembered. Not the past month, but the friendship she'd had all those years with Jack. From the time they took their first toddling steps up until the day she'd left him sitting right there in the same spot they were now, on the same quilt, listening to the same CD. Lord, how had she ever made it seven years without his friendship?

"I knew things weren't right. He'd been working late, not coming home at all some nights. But that night, he'd called and said he'd be home right after work and he wanted me to be there so we could talk, so I spent the day in the kitchen." She attempted a smile, but it didn't reach her eyes.

Jack watched the bobble out on the water; his jaw clenched.

"I met him in the living room, and he told me to sit down. He said, 'Dee, I am divorcing you. Actually, it's an annulment. As of this morning we are no longer married. I'm moving out right now. My dad will be by later today to discuss the settlement we are giving you. It's generous and will compensate you for the past seven years.' Then he got up and went up to our bedroom, packed a suitcase, and started out the front door. That's when I threw a vase across the room. It hit the door and shattered all around him. He said, 'I would have expected you to have at least gotten some class in the past seven years. Guess it's true that you can take the girl out of the gutter, but you can't take the gutter out of the girl.' "

Jack touched the scar on his face. "I remember your temper. Is that when you killed him and buried him down under the coal bin in the basement?"

"No, that's when I asked him what in the hell was going on."

"And?"

"He said Angie had come home. His precious high school sweetheart. They'd had a terrible fight and broken up when she wanted to go to France to expand her horizons seven years before. Those are his words, not mine. I'd like to expand her horizons. Straight down to have an up-close and personal visit with Lucifer himself. But anyway, when she came home, after her horizons were broadened in Europe, she went straight to Ray and he opened up his arms. I found out he'd married me on the rebound. Just three months after she'd broken up with him. Seven years later, Angie came home and . . ."

"And you'd never even heard of Angie?" Jack asked.

"Not one time. Not until Ray had his suitcase in his hands and was walking out on me. Best-kept secret in the whole world."

"So how did he annul a seven-year marriage?"

"I have no idea. It must have taken a lot of money. Angie was pregnant, though, and they wanted an instant marriage in the church. So my marriage no longer exists. I suppose it's because we didn't get married in the church but by a judge in the first courthouse we came to after we left here. I got a healthy settlement, my name back, and my choice of vehicles. I opted for the truck since I could haul my things home in it. Besides, it was the only vehicle Ray had never driven."

They watched the bobbles in comfortable silence, more peaceful than any place or any thing Dee had felt in months. She leaned back on an elbow, kept her eyes on the red-and-white ball, and didn't even mind the heat. "So what about you? Got a marriage to report in the past seven years? Remember now, I don't know anything. I didn't get anything but a three-minute Monday morning call from Tally."

"Even this past year? She called when she was in jail? How'd you know about Nanna and Poppa?"

"Yes, she's called, but she sure didn't tell me it was from jail. She'd tell me how Roxie was doing, what was going on with Mimosa and Bodine. She never mentioned she was in trouble. She did say that Mimosa was thinking about retiring, but I was shocked to see her sitting in the yard. And I knew about Nanna and Poppa because I had the Sulphur newspaper sent to me. I read the whole thing including the advertisements every single week." Dee yawned.

"No marriages in my past. Almost, but not quite," he said.

"Cold feet?"

"No, Roxie." He laughed.

"Does this story require another Coke?"

"Probably." He pulled the tab on two cans and handed her one.

"Right after Nanna died, the place was so quiet it felt like a tomb. I looked around the church and picked the most likely woman I could live with. I convinced myself I was in love. Looking back, I wanted to not be lonely, and she liked the looks of my checking account. She'd already started telling me about the house we were going to build, in Sulphur. We were going to sell the store and trailer and I was going to be the mayor or something big like that. I was beginning to get that itchy feeling that said, 'Run, Jack. Run. Run. Run.' Then one evening, Roxie came toting a big pitcher of her lemonade and poured three glasses. One for me, one for her, and one for Marla. Truth be told, I think Bodine overheard some of the conversations Marla and I were having and ratted me out."

"Oh, no!" Dee's eyes widened.

"Oh, yes. Roxie pulled up a chair and commenced talking. By the way, Marla didn't wear a hat or gloves to church. And she'd grown up in California," he said.

"At least she wasn't a Yankee," Dee said.

"No, but barely a step down. Roxie asked her if she was partial to roses and did she realize just how much work went into keeping Nanna's roses blooming all summer? Did she know about aphids and spider mites and all the things that could kill a rose overnight? She told Marla how glad she was to have a woman next door again, and she hoped she'd pop in often. Of course, she would be expected to be on the porch at sunset every evening. That was just the law of the Corner. By the time she started in on how Marla would be good friends with Tally when she got out of county for hot checks, Marla was getting that deer-in-the-headlights look. Then Bodine came in the front door and mentioned that Roxie could teach her to can vegetables and make jelly once she'd moved into the trailer. That set Roxie off on a tangent about Marla reinstating Nanna's vegetable garden and cleaning fish." Jack laughed so hard he had to stop talking.

"Jack, I am so sorry," Dee said.

"Why? It made me see Marla through their eyes. I'd built her up to be the best thing since ice cream on a stick. Thought she'd change once we were engaged and married. I even had her donning an old straw hat and going fishing every morning like Nanna did while Poppa ran the store. All it took was Roxie to show me her true colors." Jack wiped his eyes with the back of his hand.

"But weren't you mad?" Dee asked incredulously.

"Sure I was mad. Marla pitched a fit the whole way

to her little low-slung sportscar about how she'd never live next to that crazy bunch of retarded fools. I could choose them or her and I had until she started the engine to do so. Somehow, I just couldn't see leaving Buckhorn Corner."

"Ain't easy letting her be right all the time, is it?"

"She's a witch, I swear she is," Jack said. "She's got a sixth sense about things." He didn't want things to slip back into the old pattern. God knew he didn't, but somehow it was happening: he and Dee telling stories and sharing their worlds.

Dee giggled. "Roxie is still the queen of Roxie's Blessin's and Bellyachin'. I've been scared to death that she'd change while I was gone."

"Roxie won't ever change. She might change Heaven, but nothing will change her. Don't think they're bitin' tonight." Jack brought his line in and laid the rod beside the quilt. He stretched out and gazed at the stars. He'd been furious when she told him she was eloping with Ray and tried to talk her out of it, but he couldn't stay angry with her, not when she was right beside him. His world was set aright again.

She looked up at the same stars. Had it really been seven years since she'd been to the Lake of the Arbuckles to fish for catfish? In some ways it seemed like that young girl who'd taken her rebellion and rolled it into nice, fluffy dreams never existed at all. Other ways, it was only yesterday. An eternity. A blink of the eyes. Another woman who went down the yellow brick road only to find it didn't have a rainbow at the end. A broken road that only circled around and brought her back to the same place.

"Did you go to OU?" she finally asked. That had been his all-time big dream, to go to the University of Oklahoma and become the next Bill Gates.

"No, went a couple of years down to MIT. That would be Murray in Tishomingo, if you'll remember. Got an associate's degree in computer programming. By then Poppa was getting more feeble. I told myself I was just laying out a semester to help him with the store. If we'd have shut up the store, he'd have lain down and died for sure. Nanna wasn't able to drive after the first stroke, so I got up early and brought her down here, got her settled in with her fishing pole, and then went back to open the store. At noon, I'd shut it up for an hour, come get Nanna and bring her home, fix their lunch, and put her down for a nap. Then Poppa and I'd go back to the store," he said.

"You are a saint," Dee said.

"I don't think so." He smiled.

"I always envied you having a Poppa and Nanna," she admitted.

"I always envied you having Roxie and Mimosa and Tally and even Bodine when she came to live with y'all. One great big bunch of family to laugh and fight with," he said.

"But we're weird. You got to call your grandmother something neat like Nanna. I called mine Roxie and my mother Mimosa," she said.

"That's because . . ." He stopped and waited for her to catch on.

"Because only God and General Lee have titles. The rest of us have names in this family," they said in unison.

"Dysfunctional doesn't even begin to describe us, does it?" she asked.

"Neither of us came from dysfunctional families, Dee. Dysfunctional is a word that means nonworking. We grew up in eccentric families. We're not dysfunctional. We're simply crazy," Jack said.

"Ain't it the truth. So are you ever going to go back and finish your degree?" she asked.

"Have no intentions of it. Don't need to. I'm creating computer games. I just did one about the mafia. You know the old arcade games where the bad guys get shot up and the good guys win? Something like that, only on a CD. Three of us started up a little company when we were in college. I do what I want. I sell bread and milk to the campers. Create games and sit on the back porch with Roxie and the family in the evenings. Do a little fishing? Eat a little catfish. Listen to Floyd Cramer when the mood strikes me. Or Billy Ray or Patsy Cline if I'm in the mood. If I'm not, I sit on the porch and watch the lightning bugs in the evenings or the school bus pick up Bodine in the mornings while I have my coffee. It's a good life, Dee. Uncomplicated and free." He shut his eyes and snored lightly.

Free. Happy. But where did she fit into the picture? Sure, she had enough money from the interest on her settlement to live comfortably, but is that what she wanted? To be content to watch Bodine get on the school bus? To be fishing with Jack when she was sixty? She'd have to think about it later, she thought, as she rolled over on her side and watched Jack doze. Just before her eyes got so heavy she couldn't keep them open any longer, she was grateful that he and Marla hadn't married. Right then she needed his friendship far more than that hussy needed his money.

Roxie was sitting in the kitchen at daybreak when they came wandering in, sleep still sticking to them. "Good morning. You going to make an honest woman out of my granddaughter? Kept her out all night."

"No, I'm not going to make an honest woman of her, Roxie. She's too wild for the long haul. Never know when she's liable to run off with the next smooth-talking fool that turns her head. Can't trust the woman. She gave up on the fish and went to sleep. And she drank Coke right out of the can. I had a glass right there but she wouldn't use it." Jack's eyes twinkled.

"I knew it. We'll just have to retrain her. Is there going to be baggage for me to have to take care of in nine months?" Roxie pulled pink foam rollers out of her bright red hair.

Dee shot her a look meant to freeze her on the spot. "Roxie!"

"No, ma'am," he said.

"You two stop talking about me like I'm not here. I fell asleep the same as you." She pointed to Jack.

"You slept with Jack?" Bodine asked from the doorway, rubbing her eyes.

"No, I did not!" Dee threw up her hands.

"Did too!" Jack slapped at her, the wind off his hand fanning across her arm.

"Yes, Bodine, we slept together. On a quilt, but that's exactly what we did. We slept," Dee said.

"Well, it's a good thing this is Sunday and we're going to church. You can pray for forgiveness for your sins. I think I may be a nun today and wear a black dress and one of those white things on my head. What's for breakfast?"

"Whatever you want, honey. And there are no nuns in the Baptist church. You will wear your new green sprigged dress and straw hat, so don't be thinkin' I'll give in and let you dress in that pilgrim outfit so you'll look like a nun. Individuality stops on Sunday." Roxie pulled the last roller out of her hair with a grimace. "Go tell Mimosa to get up. She's got to rat my hair up and fix it for church."

"I'll get on home and grab a shower. Meet y'all back here at ten?" He looked at Roxie.

"We'll be ready. You bring the van, and we'll only have to take one car. It's your day to decide on where we're eating dinner. Then we'll go see Tally. I got a basket of stuff to take to her," Roxie said.

"Thanks for sleeping with me," Jack threw over his shoulder as he hurried out the back door.

"Roxie, I didn't sleep with him, not in the Biblical sense of the word," Dee protested.

"Honey, I wouldn't care if you did. Jack's a good person. Knows where his roots are and isn't ashamed of who he is. Don't go dillydallyin' around thinkin' he'll be there until eternity. He was in love with you in high school, but he was too shy to let you know it. You probably could fan those fires a little bit."

"Roxie! Jack was and is my friend. He didn't have a crush on me. Not ever. I would have known."

"Like you knew that man who blacked your eye because you didn't jump when he told you to? Did he ever do it again?"

"No, he didn't. I wouldn't have stayed with him if he'd been abusive. It was a one-time thing and we were arguing really bad. It got out of hand."

"And you married him anyway. For a year, every time the phone rang I expected it to be the police telling me to come claim your body, or else telling me you'd killed him. Before I answered it I prayed that he was in the morgue and not you, but we don't need to talk about that. Right now, I'm going to make breakfast. You get upstairs and take a shower. I put a pair of black gloves up there on your bed beside the hat. They're lace, so that makes up for the fact that it's still legally summer. It's all right to wear patent leather and black lace before Labor Day. And darlin', hold your head up high when you walk into that church. Pride and dignity are our trademarks," Roxie said.

"Then why did you paint the house this gawdawful color? There's not a bit of pride or dignity in it," Dee said.

"Dee, God made the cardinal, and there isn't a bird out there with more pride or dignity than the cardinal and it's bright red. You got about fifteen minutes before breakfast, so you'd better hurry up." Roxie pointed to the gently curving staircase.

Pride and dignity. Dee almost giggled as she made her way upstairs to the family quarters. The house had been built as a boardinghouse fifty years ago. Five bedrooms upstairs for the family that had four sons. Ten rooms on a wing that stretched out from the dining room for boarders. Eight bedrooms. Two bathrooms. His and hers. A dining room that could easily seat twenty people. A kitchen with two stoves and a mammoth-sized refrigerator. Roxie had paid for it with a very small portion of what Henry had left when he died, back when Mimosa was four years old. The same year the engineers opened the gates and the Lake of the Arbuckles flooded more than two thousand acres of land. Located on Highway 177 and the corner where the campers turned down to that part of the lake known as the Buckhorn, it was one of three white elephants in the county. Molly Branson, known as Granny Branson, ran one of the others. Etta Cahill was the proprietor of the third one. Three old places that had been the place to stay in their day. At least the other two were legitimately white.

After Dee showered she slipped into her black dress and picked up the gaudiest hat she'd ever seen. Ray would hate it. He'd refuse to go to church with her wearing that monstrosity. A grin brightened her whole face as she picked up a hat pin with a big gold button on the end and shoved it in the back.

She was ready to face the world.

Chapter Three

Forget about sneaking in and sitting on the back pew just to satisfy Roxie. Oh, no, the Hooper family, plus Jack, sat together in the second pew on the left, just like they'd always done. Bodine led the way, a princess in her green-sprigged dress with a wide, darker green satin ribbon sash, pretty white sandals, white short gloves with a tiny covered button to tighten them up at the wrist, and an enormous floppy straw hat with the same green ribbon encircling the crown and tied in a bow at the back with streamers hanging to her waist. Roxie had used mousse in Bodine's naturally curly, light-brown hair, and it looked as if she'd just gotten a spiral perm at the beauty shop. There were women who would die for hair like Bodine's.

Mimosa followed Bodine. Dressed in a cute pink suit with a skirt that stopped at midthigh, she wore a fluff of something in her short hair that barely resembled a hat. It's a wonder Roxie ever let her out of the house. But she did have pink gloves with white daisies, so that would probably keep her out of hell's heat for one day. Even Lucifer had more self-respect than to let someone wearing pink gloves trimmed with white daisies inside the fiery gates.

Dee held her head high. If she hadn't, the red hat with the black lace and illusion trim with the big bow on the side would have fallen off. The disgrace of such a thing would have put the whole Hooper family on probation for a hundred years. She wasn't totally sure St. Peter would even let them peek at the Pearly Gates with a demerit like that on their sheet. She felt the glaring stares of every woman in the church. Thank goodness Jack was right behind her or she might have thrown her hat at the altar, turned around, and lit a shuck for . . . she couldn't think of a single place she'd go, suddenly.

"You are beautiful today. I forgot to tell you that when I picked you ladies up. I was spellbound by your beauty," Jack said as they waited for Roxie. Nobody sat down until Roxie arrived. It was downright disrespectful and bordered on a mortal sin.

"I look like an overdressed country hick or someone you'd pick up off the streets in this getup. Next week I'm going shopping for the tiniest hat I can find. Maybe just a bow on a headband so I can fake it like Mimosa," she whispered.

"Pick up off the streets, huh? I didn't pay you for last

night." He pulled a quarter from his pocket and placed it in her hand.

"Some help you are," she hissed.

"Made you smile though, didn't I? Really, you look beautiful," he whispered.

"And you are a wonderful liar."

Roxie took her place, and they all sat down at the same time. Roxie wore her trademark: ruffles, and lots of them. Around a plunging neckline as well as the hem of her red dress, belted in the middle with a wide white sash that matched white three-inch spike-heeled Prada pumps, white gloves, and a white hat decorated with red roses. Her ratted and sprayed red hair peeked out from the edges of the hat, giving testimony that Mimosa had created a wonderful hairdo that morning.

Dee touched Jack's arm and leaned toward his ear. "Thank you for the compliment. You don't look so shabby yourself this morning, but you don't have to wear a hat and gloves."

"Roxie would kill me if I wore a hat in church." He leaned over to whisper in her ear.

The warmth of his breath on the soft skin of her neck sent a shiver all the way down to her toes, encased in black patent leather two-inch pumps. She told herself that the shiver was caused by his 98.6 temperature on her skin that had been chilled by the air-conditioned church. She wasn't going to trust any man, not even Jack.

"Shhhh." Roxie tapped Jack on the leg and put a finger over her lips. "You two got things to say, you can say them after church."

A little lady with freshly styled hair somewhere between purple and blue leaned over from the third pew and touched Roxie on the shoulder. "Is that Dee? Is she home for good or just a-visiting?"

Roxie's red painted mouth broke into a smile. "Yes, it's Dee. She's home for good. Tally will be with us in a few weeks."

"That's good, Roxie. That's real good. I'll be sure to speak to her after church," the lady said.

"Shhh," Dee leaned forward and mouthed to Roxie, putting a finger on her own red lips.

Roxie shot her a mean look and tilted her chin an inch higher.

The beginning hymn was sung. Afterward, special music was delivered by none other than Marla Pritchard, who presented a moving contemporary gospel piece. The sermon was delivered and the offering plate passed. Roxie put in a twenty-dollar bill. Inflation had reared its ugly head, Dee thought, because seven years ago Roxie laid a ten on the plate every Sunday. Jack put in a folded check. Dee dropped her quarter inside the velvet bag.

"And there was a widow lady who gave her all," she whispered to Jack.

"Bless you my child," he whispered back.

The invitational in which the whole congregation sang every last word of "Jesus Is Calling" netted no sinners who wanted to be redeemed. So the preacher announced that the Reynolds children would be hosting a golden anniversary party for their parents on Thursday night in the fellowship hall. The Andersons had a new baby girl named Hannah Elisabeth, who would be dedicated next Sunday. And Marla Pritchard and Jeff O'Toole were announcing their engagement. The wedding would be a Christmas affair, and all friends and family were invited.

The preacher gave the benediction.

Dee whispered in Jack's ear as they stood up and waited for Roxie to lead them out of the building. "I'm so sorry, darlin'. It must be painful to see old Jeff O'Toole cheat you out of the love of your life."

Jack placed a hand over his heart. "Oh, it is. I may never get over it. Want to go fishing this afternoon and help me forget the torment tearing my heart out?"

"I'm taking a nap this afternoon," Dee told him. "You snored all night and kept me from getting a good night's sleep."

Marla stopped Roxie when they were halfway up the aisle. "Oh, Roxie, darlin', is this your granddaughter who was in jail?"

"No, this is the one who had the good grace to kill her husband and get away with it. You know: no body, no evidence. I trained her well," Roxie said.

Dee smiled and held out her gloved hand. "And you must be Marla. I'm so glad to make your acquaintance. You sing like an angel, darlin'. Do you do weddings and funerals?"

"Of course," Marla said. "I'm even singing at my own wedding. Jeff insisted."

"I will remember that. One never knows when they'll need a singer," Dee said.

"Yes, well, I see Jeff waving at me. I must go now. Oh, hello, Jack. I didn't see you there." She extended her left hand. A diamond the size of a good big hailstone on a wide platinum band sparkled.

Jack bent low and brushed a kiss across her fingertips. "Congratulations, Marla. I hope you and Jeff are very happy."

"Oh, we will be," Marla sniffed dramatically. "So glad to meet you, Tally."

"No, darlin', that's the one in jail for hot checks. I'm Dee, as in Delylah. You know, the one in the Bible who outwitted the strong man, Samson. That's me. Dee. The one who married the man whose body they'll never find."

"Yes, well, I'll be seeing you all." She shuddered. The whole bunch of those Hooper women was crazy as loons. As long as Jack lived next door to that batch of witches, he'd never find a bride.

"Well done, my child. And you've only been home two days. Couldn't have done better if I'd coached you," Roxie said out the side of her mouth.

"It's like riding a bicycle, Roxie. You never forget how to perform in a catfight. Now where did you say we're having lunch? I'm starving. They do have fried okra, don't they?"

"Honey, any restaurant worth its salt has okra. How about Jewel's today, Roxie?" Jack asked.

"Sounds good to me. I could eat a big plate of barbecue, and they know how to make it," Roxie said.

"But I wanted a Sonic hamburger with cheese tots," Bodine said.

"Next week, it's your turn," Mimosa told her. "This week it's Jack's. You can order a burger at Jewel's, and I'm sure they'll melt some cheese on your tater tots. After we visit Tally, we'll go to Braum's for banana splits."

Dee all but moaned. In a week, her jeans would be too tight.

Jack held the door of the van. Roxie crawled in first and sat on the second seat with Mimosa right beside her. Bodine took the back seat. He slid the panel door shut and opened the passenger door for Dee. The whole town would see her riding shotgun, and the rumors would have it next week that not only had she murdered her husband and disposed of his body, she was now keeping company with Jack. The story would also have it that he deserved it after the shabby way he'd treated Marla.

"Okay, girls, it's time to take off the hats and gloves." Roxie was already removing hers as she spoke.

"But I thought I'd wear mine all day and maybe even to bed tonight. Jack said I looked stunning." Dee couldn't believe she was teasing. She'd figured she'd be walking around in a daze for years. And here she was laughing after only forty-eight hours back in Sulphur, Oklahoma. It all went to show the power of a family and one good old fishing friend could have in her life.

"Of course you do, but you're not ruining my new hat by sleeping in it. Jack thinks you are just as stunning in your old fishing hat. The one with all the lures and hooks in it. You can sleep in that," Roxie said.

"Do you?" Dee looked at him while they were waiting for the traffic light to turn green.

"Of course, I do." He grinned.

"You lie so well. I swear you'd think you grew up next door to Roxie."

Dee removed the hat pin and handed the fancy hat back to Roxie. "Why do we have to wear a hat and gloves if we're just going to take them off the minute the last amen is said?"

"God expects women to be women, and General Lee would be disappointed in his ladies of the South if we didn't keep the standard," Bodine recited the words verbatim.

"Yes, ma'am." Dee nodded seriously. Bodine would be as warped as the rest of them by the time she graduated high school, but when she chose her broken roads, she could retrace her footsteps and come right back home.

Roxie had barbecue. Bodine ordered a burger and cheese fries. Mimosa opted for roast beef with potatoes and carrots on the side. Dee studied the menu, then ordered a hamburger with mustard and all the works, an order of fried okra, a bowl of red beans, and a plate of cornbread. Jack echoed Dee's order.

"I missed this kind of food," Dee said.

"You mean they don't even have hamburgers in that foreign country where you went? I'm not about to go there, then. Did they have cheese tots?" Bodine asked.

"Yes, they have burgers and I suppose there's some place you can order cheese tots, but they don't serve red beans except at Cracker Barrel and Ray hated eating at that place. Said it was absolutely bohemian to eat that close to other people." Dee picked up the catsup bottle and laid a nice layer over her fries. She even dipped a piece of fried okra in it and shut her eyes when she popped it in her mouth.

"We'll have no more mention of that man's name in my presence," Roxie informed her. "It'll ruin my barbecue for sure."

"Mimosa, I can't believe you've been home a whole month, and there's not been one semi roaring down the lane." Jack deftly changed the subject, putting Mimosa in the spotlight and giving Dee some breathing room.

"I'm retired, honey. Last week I met a trucker in the Ardmore Wal-Mart store, back there in that little coffee shop part of it. We talked for an hour, and I didn't even feel the pull to go back on the road. I'm thinking of enrolling in that cosmetology school down there this fall. Put in a little shop right here in Sulphur when I get finished," Mimosa said.

"Sounds like a plan to me," Roxie said.

"Then you wouldn't mind being alone all day?" Mimosa asked.

"No, I wouldn't mind staying alone all day," Roxie snapped. "I told you, just because you're tired of trucking, don't be thinking you're a martyr coming home to take care of your mother. I'm not senile. I'm not feeble. And I've stayed alone in the house before without wetting my pants or forgetting where the kitchen is." She accentuated every word with a stab of her fork toward Mimosa.

"Then that's what I'm doing," Mimosa declared.

"You should be good at it. Just don't let them tell you that ratted hair is out of style. I like my hair teased up, not lying flat against my head like a boy's," Roxie said.

"You looking forward to school starting up, Bodine?" Jack kept the spotlight moving.

"Of course she is. Get back in with her little friends," Roxie said.

"Yes, I am. I think it's a great waste of time to go to school, but I can't get on one of those space shuttles and go to the moon without an education. Southern belles are fast becoming a thing of the past, you know. Us women folks have to learn how to survive in a man's world."

"Yes, ma'am, I agree. The charms of a southern woman are about to be put at the top of the endangered species list, but I'm sure. What do you intend to do when you get to the moon?" he asked in all seriousness.

"Why, I intend to have an Orange Julius and go to the nearest mall and see if they sell parasols." Her face lit up in a smile, showing two front teeth that she'd be a couple of years growing into.

"Take them a little charm, then?" Jack asked.

"Of course. Why else would anyone want to go up there anyway? I don't even like green cheese. It smells gawdawful," Bodine said.

"You want me to wash your mouth out? They got a bathroom in this place with lots of soap," Roxie said.

"No, Roxie, I apologize. Tally is a bad influence on me. Just thinking about going to see her, why, I can't stop those bad words from sneaking right out of my mouth," Bodine told her.

Dee suppressed a giggle. Jack reached under the table and squeezed her knee. He'd done that a million times in the past, but never had it affected her like it did right then. Her stomach went all mushy and if she'd had to utter a complete sentence or die, she'd have had to ask for a blindfold and a firing squad. It had to be the fact that she was back home in the bosom of her family, and—crazy, weird bunch that they were—they still were family.

She chewed slowly and remembered the night she told Jack she was leaving the next day, both of them just out of high school. Eighteen years old and green as a pair of newly hatched garden snakes. He'd tried his best to talk her out of it. Said she should at least wait a month to see if she still loved Ray then. He'd reminded her of the time Ray had hit her. But she would not listen. No sir, she was going to Pennsylvania where a perfect family awaited her, where she'd be a flawless little corporate wife. She shook away the memories and came back to the present, enjoyed every bite of the hamburger, and had the last piece of cornbread on her plate for dessert. She sliced it open, slathered on butter and covered it with honey, then ate it with a fork like it was a piece of cake.

After they'd all finished, Jack picked up the tab and

drove them to the county jail. They found Tally waiting in the fenced yard.

Her eyes widened when she saw Dee. She crossed the yard in a few easy long strides and wrapped her sister into her arms. "I was going to call you tomorrow, and here you are. I'm so glad to see you. Did you divorce him or kill him?"

"He annulled me," Dee told her.

Tally was eight inches taller than Dee, had a magnificent head of thick, naturally blond hair and the bluest eyes in all of Oklahoma. Her waist was small, her bosom big; her legs went on forever. If she could have sung, she would have made a stunning addition to the country music industry, but her voice was thin and nasal.

"How does one annul a marriage after seven years?" Tally asked.

"Money greases machines," Dee answered.

"Well, God will forgive you for that one. He was a horse's rear end, and you're better off without him. Hey, Roxie, they said I could have three weeks off for good behavior so could you send someone after me next Saturday?" Tally said.

"I'll come get you," Mimosa said.

"Thanks. Now come and tell me everything that's gone on this week. Bodine, you look like a princess." Tally drew her daughter to her side and hugged her.

"Of course I do," Bodine said. "But princesses can't say bad words. Roxie threatened to wash my mouth out with soap. Right there in a public place."

"Bodine! What Roxie says is the law!" Tally shook her finger at her daughter.

"Yes, ma'am, but you say those words. I heard you call Dee's husband worse than that."

"Yes, but he made our Dee sad."

Dee sat down on a bench next to a picnic table. "How'd you know that?"

"Oh, honey, I'm the older sister. I can tell by the tone of your voice when you're sad."

"Is she sad now?" Jack asked.

"Lord, no. How could anyone be sad with something as pretty as you to look at? Or eating Roxie's cooking? Or fishing the Buckhorn? She's as happy as a piglet in a fresh wallow. I would've given her a gun and an alibi if she'd wanted to finish that business off out there before he decided to pay his way out of a marriage," Tally said.

Dee changed the subject. "So what are you going to do when you get out?"

"I'm going to college. Roxie said so. I'm thirty-one years old. I've tried singing. I've tried about everything. Nothing worked. So Roxie said I'm going to Murray State College and getting an education. After I finish two years there, then I'm going to East Central in Ada and becoming a teacher," Tally said.

"No more bad checks," Mimosa muttered.

"No, ma'am. Roxie done broke me from sucking eggs on that issue. No more bad checks. No more lazy husbands. Although I only had one of those. You kind of outdid me on that issue, Mimosa," Tally said.

Roxie threw up her hands. "Thank God you didn't follow in her footsteps."

"What are you going to do?" Tally asked Dee. "You only got one mistake under your belt."

"But it's a big one, isn't it?" Dee patted Roxie's knee.

"Yes, but like the preacher said, I am a generous woman and I forgive my offspring their mistakes. I might put out a contract on that sorry man who hurt you, but I will forgive him while he's bleeding to death," Roxie said.

"Let's don't kill him," Dee said.

"Then forgiveness will be a long time coming. I'll just have to outlive him and then forgive him when I lay a wilted rose on his casket, because I can't forgive that man as long as he's got air in his lungs," Roxie declared.

Tally looked at Dee. "So you didn't answer my question. What are you going to do?"

"I'm not going to do a blessed thing but drink lemonade in the evenings while I watch the sunset. I might do a little fishing. I might take care of the rosebushes and help with the vegetable garden and cook a few meals if Roxie will let me in the kitchen, but I'm not doing anything until after Christmas. Then I'll decide what I want to do," Dee said.

"Bravo," Tally said. "The prodigal comes home with a plan."

"I rather like it," Jack said.

Dee turned quickly to find him staring at her, his eyes sparkling and a grin showing off his perfect white teeth.

"Me too." Bodine added her approval. "That way Jack and Dee will both be there when I get off the bus."

"Yes, ma'am, we surely will," Dee said.

Tally looked at her grandmother. "Roxie?"

"Rules is rules. You've had enough chances, Tally. You don't get to laze around the garden and the fishing hole. You've got to get some direction to your life. Both you and Mimosa. Dee can have her time to get settled and get her heart back in working order," Roxie declared.

Tally stuck her tongue out at Dee.

Dee did the same, right back.

Bodine tattled.

Jack roared.

Mimosa pretended she didn't see a thing.

Roxie bit the inside of her lip to keep from laughing. Her family was home and safe. She was the grand matriarch, sitting on her throne once again. Today the blessin's outweighed the bellyachin'.

Chapter Four

"Halle-blessed-lujah, I am home," Tally said dramatically as she flung open the front door and stepped inside the house.

Roxie came out of the kitchen, wiping her hands on a tea towel. "And tell me you're not going away again?"

"No, ma'am, I am not. This is heaven. I'm going upstairs for a long hot bath, then I'm going to fix a glass of iced tea and sit out under the shade trees with no fences between me and freedom," she said.

"You're going upstairs for a long bath, and then we'll have supper. We'll all sit on the back porch together and watch the sun set after we eat like we always do, then you can sit out under the shade trees until midnight if you want to," Roxie said.

"A good cold Dr Pepper then, while I soak?" Tally asked.

"Dee, honey, pour up a cold Dr Pepper in a glass and take it up to Tally," Roxie yelled toward the kitchen.

"Yes, ma'am." Dee came out, an oversized bib apron over her cutoff denim shorts and faded red tank top, barefoot, her hair held back with a plastic head band. "Welcome back home, Tally. Here, let me help you with those sacks."

"Honey, I can carry the Wal-Mart Samsonite up to my room if you'll just bring me a something cold to sip on while I soak. Roxie says I can't laze around until after supper," Tally said.

"Wal-Mart Samsonite?" Dee asked.

"That's what those blue plastic bags are called in redneck language," Tally laughed.

Bodine appeared at the top of the stairs. "We might be rednecks, but as soon as I can find a frog to put in my witch's brew, I'm going to make a potion that will turn us all into sophisticated millionaires. Can we go to the Buckhorn and find a frog? I need a real one. Not an old brown toad."

"Of course, honey. As soon as I have a long, soaking bath, we'll go find a frog. Bet there's one down by the Buckhorn. After supper, we'll drive down there and see what we can find," Tally said.

"Can we ride our bicycles rather than drive?"

"No, we cannot. That's five miles and my legs aren't up to that kind of punishment today," Tally told her.

"I'll get the Dr Pepper," Dee said.

"I'll be waiting in the tub. I'll be the one with bubbles up to my chin. Bodine, get that recipe out and make sure a frog is all you need. Maybe you'll need the skeleton of a bass or a pilfered catfish head from a barbed wire fence." Tally grinned.

"I'll go check," Bodine said seriously.

When the water pipes stopped rattling, Dee carried a chilled can of Dr Pepper and an empty glass up to her sister. The bathroom door was wide open, the curtains covering the window tucked up over the curtain rod. Hot afternoon sun streamed in through the spotless window pane.

Tally opened one eye a slit. "Ahh. Light. Bubbles. Cold soda pop. The world is a good place to be."

Dee poured enough Dr Pepper in the glass to swish it around and handed it to her sister, who reached out through the bubbles to gulp it down in one sip.

"Now for the good stuff," Tally said.

Dee put the sweating can in her hands and she tilted it back. "Don't you dare tell Roxie I'm drinking from the can. She'll put me back in jail for those last three weeks."

"Wouldn't think of it. She tried to make me marry Jack just because we fished all night and drank from the can." Dee set the empty glass on the vanity and pulled the bench out, settling down and entwining one leg around the other. "Tell me, weren't you mad at her for letting them take you to jail? That's a whole year out of your life."

"Oh, sister, mad ain't even the word for it. I paced that cell for a month. Refused to come out on Sunday to see any of them, even Bodine. But Roxie came every week and brought a sack full of goodies. Pecan pies. Chocolate cakes. Magazines. Books. A Game Boy. Even a television set for my cell. On the fifth Sunday I went out in the yard to wait, to give her a piece of my mind."

Tally finished off the Dr Pepper and stretched out in the old claw-foot bathtub. "I'm going to stay here until all the bubbles go flat and my skin is as wrinkled as an old prune."

"What happened?" Dee asked.

"I gave her a good-sized chunk of my mind. Told her she would have never missed the money to pay my fines and pick up the checks," Tally said.

"And then?" Dee asked.

"She said I was right. She wouldn't have missed the money, but a year inside would be good for me. To think about what direction my life was going. I wrote the checks to cover my gambling debts, Dee. I'm an addict. Can't go anywhere near those Indian casinos. Took me a year of thinking, but it won't happen again. Roxie also said that she wouldn't be around forever to raise Bodine and sometime or other, I'd need to pick up the reins and take care of my daughter. That really sobered me up. I figured Roxie was born right after one of those big wars, not one or two, or even the northern aggression, but one in the Old Testament that the preacher talks about. Maybe when the Israelites went in to conquer the Promised Land. And I also figured she'd be the last one to leave the earth when all the nations pull out their nukes and start playing hardball. The thought that she might not be here when we get into trouble scared the bejesus out of me."

"So you really are going to school this semester?" Dee asked.

"I really am. That's one of the reasons they let me out early. I'll begin school Monday. Bodine goes back that same day, and Mimosa starts cosmetology school. It'll be a tomb around here after the weekend. You might go stark raving mad," she teased.

"I don't think so. I'm barely settled in, and besides, I need a while to get my head on straight. What are you going to do when you graduate? By then Bodine will be fifteen," Dee asked.

"When I get finished, I'm going to take Bodine with me wherever I can find a job. If it's within driving distance, I'll probably stay right here and do what Mimosa keeps mouthing about—take care of Roxie if she ever does need me. But if it's far away, I'm going to stop playing around and take care of the daughter I produced. That's something Mimosa hasn't ever done, so maybe Roxie did teach the two of us something, even if it's taken me a long time to figure it out. Now what about you?"

"You just wasted one year. I wasted seven."

"Oh, honey, if we're totaling, I think I can claim thirteen. But the last one isn't wasted. It's probably the most profitable of them all. What about you and Jack? I saw the way he was lookin' at you last Sunday."

"Jack is my friend and always has been. I didn't realize how much I'd missed him until I came back and found him right here. But that's all there is, Tally. Honest. He means too much to me to ruin what we've got with romance."

"I see." Tally rested her head on the back of the tub.

"Don't fall asleep and drown. I'm going back to the kitchen. Roxie is making a big supper and has invited Jack. Celebration, you know. I've been pulled out of the raging fires of hell. You've come to your senses. Mimosa is retiring. It's like Christmas in July."

"Don't open up that Christmas present called retiring just yet. The day Mimosa really retires is when they'll probably start tossing around those nukes. Is Roxie cooking ham and baked beans?"

Dee put her finger to her lips. "It's a surprise. And banana nut cake and hot rolls."

"Blessin's today," Tally giggled.

"Seems that way." Dee left Tally to grow wrinkled all alone.

Supper was served in the dining room with the good dishes and crystal goblets. Roxie sat at the head of the table. She'd dressed in a white pantsuit with a wide, shiny gold belt and big gold hoop earrings. Tally, Bodine, and Mimosa sat on her left; Dee and Jack on her right. A queen holding court over a table of ham, baked beans, fried okra, sliced tomatoes, potato salad, and iced tea. Banana nut cake and homemade ice cream waited in the kitchen.

Jack passed the beans to his right and took the bowl of okra with his left. "May I say all you ladies look beautiful tonight? Roxie, darlin', will you run away with me to Mexico after supper?"

Roxie laughed out loud. "Jack, you've been a charmer since you were a baby. That's not your hormones talkin', it's your starvin' stomach."

"Then how about you, Mimosa? We can get one of those big old RVs and you'll feel like you're back on the road. Surely you've got ramblin' fever by now."

Mimosa sipped her iced tea, her eyes glittering. "Let me think about it a minute? No, I'll have to pass. Seen enough roads and country, but I'm flattered that you'd find an old woman like me interesting enough to elope with."

"Darlin', the day Mimosa Hooper is old is the day the world comes to a screeching halt." Jack raised his eyebrows, flirting blatantly.

"It's my turn?" Bodine piped up.

"Bodine, my sweet princess-slash-pirate-slash-witch, will you hurry and grow up so we can run away together?" Jack never took his eyes off the eleven-year-old girl across the table.

Bodine followed Mimosa's lead. "Let me think about it? No, Jack, I wouldn't want to break your heart, but I'm going to go to the moon, not Mexico. Besides, you're just too old for me."

"Ouch." Jack frowned. "Do you think I'll be forgetting where I live and needing a walking cane anytime soon?"

"Could be," Bodine sighed. "Of course, not until after Roxie dies, though. She'll keep everyone alive and well until she dies. Then I expect you'd better be real nice to Dee because she'll have to help you find your walking cane."

"Roxie isn't going to die," Mimosa said.

"I will if I want to," Roxie said seriously.

"Okay, enough about dying," Dee said. "That's not a nice conversation for Tally to have to listen to on her first day home. Let's talk about something more pleasant. Jack, did you get the roses watered today?"

"Of course," he said. "See, Bodine is right. You're already taking care of my memory problems. You'll have to remind me every day to water the roses, to eat, to take a bath, to sit on the porch and watch the sun set."

"Oh, hush." She slapped at him.

He caught her hand midair and what passed between them electrified the room.

She jerked her hand free from his. It wasn't happening. She'd fight any physical attraction she had to Jack to the last breath. She'd never, ever put their friendship in jeopardy. Men could only be trusted until a prettier skirt tail walked past. However, friendship was a different matter. She could trust Jack with anything . . . as long as he stayed on the friendship side of the barbed-wire fence called life. When he crossed that fence and into a new category, he wouldn't be a bit better than Ray had been.

"You sure got a funny look on your face, Dee. Is the okra burned or the tea not sweet enough?" Tally asked.

"No, the okra and the tea are fine. Just thinking, that's all."

"There will be no more thinking at the table," Bodine

issued the order in her best imitation of Roxie. "Now Jack, you have to flirt with Tally. It's her special day, and you haven't flirted with her yet."

Jack smiled brightly at Tally. "My dear, you are as lovely as a spring rose tonight in that pretty pink dress. I do declare I don't believe I've seen anything more gorgeous since before the war of northern aggression. Would you consider taking a walk with me after supper into the gardens?"

Bodine nodded appreciatively.

"Why, darlin', I would be delighted after our evening on the back porch. But alas, I cannot, for you see I have given my word that I will go with my daughter, who is a witch," she whispered the last few words. "Please don't tell anyone, we would hate for the townsfolk to drive five miles out here to burn her at the stake. It's just too dang hot to build a fire tonight. Anyway, I have pledged that I will take Miss Bodine Hooper down to the lake to see about finding a real frog that she needs to put in her brew. You see, we Hooper women must be changed into proper ladies. Bodine is working on a potion to turn us into socialites."

"They don't burn witches at the stake anymore. They stone them to death. That's what I learned in my witches book. Roxie, please pass the baked beans."

"We could fish while we wait on just the right frog to hop up on the bank and ask you to kiss him," Tally said.

Bodine put her hand over her mouth. "I'm not kissing a frog. Yuk!"

"Then you will have to give up on finding one," Mimosa said. "I believe the potion can only be made by tossing a frog into the black cauldron that has been kissed by the lips of fairest maiden in Murray County."

Bodine eyed her grandmother warily. "You're not a witch, so what do you know about making a potion?"

"Oh, but honey, that's where you are wrong. All the Hooper women are witches. Ask Roxie. She's the one who taught us." Mimosa grinned.

Roxie helped herself to another slice of ham. "Yes, that's me. Trainer of witches. Buy Wal-Mart costumes when they're eighty or ninety percent off the marked-down price, and it turns princesses to witches."

"Roxie, did your momma buy you costumes at Wal-Mart?" Bodine asked.

"Of course she did, sugar. Or at least she would have if there had been a Wal-Mart back then. Now finish your beans or there'll be no banana cake for the best of the Hooper witches," Roxie told her.

"Hooper witches. Roxie, how did we all get to have the Hooper name? Sally Jo, my friend at church, she says her grandmother's name is Granny Freeman and that's different from her momma's name," Bodine asked.

Dee and Tally both giggled at the same time.

Roxie shook her finger toward them. "Dee, drink some tea and wipe that grin off your face. Southern ladies don't show their teeth when they smile and they sure don't do it with okra stuck on them."

Dee clamped her mouth shut and winked at Tally. Both remembered the day they'd asked the same question.

"Well?" Bodine asked impatiently.

"It's like this. I was born in Mississippi, and my name was Roxanna Delight O'Shay. I married your great-grandfather, who was Henry Clay Hooper, and we moved out here when he got into the oil business," Roxie said.

"I know all that, Roxie. What I want to know is how we all got the same name, Hooper?" Bodine said.

"And like a sweet little girl, you will let your elder answer the question in the way she sees fit. So sit there and be quiet." Roxie gave her a look that silenced her immediately.

Bodine smoothed the front of her sundress and waited patiently. She didn't fool Tally, who saw the stiffness in her spine and the way she toyed with her napkin under the table. Bodine was bored, restless to be on her way to a new adventure concerning the trapping of a green frog, and sorry as the devil that she'd asked the question.

"So Henry Hooper and I got married, and the only child we produced was your grandmother, Mimosa De-light. I always loved that word. It reminded me of soft southern Mississippi summer days when the mimosa trees would be in bloom. Their petals all soft and pink. Their leaves all feathery and feminine. So that's the name I wanted for my daughter and Henry said that was fine, as long as the boys had good strong names. There weren't any more children after Mimosa, though, and Henry died when she was four. Then she grew up and ran away with a truck driver. The next year she brought Tally, your mother, back here for me to raise, since truck drivin' didn't have room for a baby bed or diapers. Her husband's name was not Hooper. I don't remember what that man's name was, too many husbands and too much water under the bridge since then. But Tally was being raised up in a Hooper house so I went to the judge and had her birth certificate changed to Tallulah Delight Hooper.

"That was too much name for me so I just called her Tally. Then six years later and at least a couple of husbands, Mimosa called me from the hospital to tell me she'd had another daughter. I told her if she was bringing her home to me, she'd better just put Hooper on the birth certificate. I wasn't having a bunch of mongrels in my house. If they were going to live here, they'd be Hoopers. So she named the baby Delylah Loretta Hooper. Said it was for Delilah in the Bible but spelled it a little different, and the Loretta was for none other than the great Loretta Lynn. Then your mother grew up and married some guitar-picking, long-haired feller and ran off to Nashville with him. Ten months later she calls me up and says that she can't raise this baby girl. Rules is rules. I told her if she was going to bring the puppy home, it was going to be a Hooper. I didn't care what that long-haired feller said about the baby having his name. If he wanted it to have his name, then he could do the three o'clock feedings and buy the Pampers. Changed his mind right quick. And that's why we are all Hoopers in this household. Only you are the last of the Hoopers, Miss Bodine. When you grow up and find a husband, you're going to raise your own puppies."

"But what would my name be if my father had stayed around and bought the Pampers?" Bodine asked.

Roxie raised an eyebrow. "Tally?"

Without blinking and with a straight face, Tally said, "Your biological father's name was Wallason Kadellosonovitch. His singing name was Wally Kadell. But your name would have been Bodine Delight Kadellosonovitch."

Bodine was horrified. "Thank God you made her name me Hooper. That name sounds like a load of pure horse—"

"Bodine!" Mimosa exclaimed before the child could complete her sentence.

Dee buried her face in her napkin and laughed until her ribs ached. It had been years since so many emotions had run through her body and soul. Friendship. Physical attraction. Family ties. Bodine's bad mouth. Roxie's queendom. Throw it all in the blender for five minutes and presto, giggles deluxe.

Jack tried to maintain his composure, but his handsome face disintegrated into a roar when he saw Dee's shoulders begin to heave. Bodine was more like Dee than she'd ever be like Tally. But then Dee had been around the first four formative years of her life. Jack remembered when Dee got her mouth washed with a soapy rag for saying bad words, and it seemed like she was just about Bodine's age when they rolled out her mouth with the least provocation.

Roxie's mouth quivered, but she kept the laughter at bay. "Am I going to get the Ivory soap? Even if it is funny, Bodine Hooper, you are not to talk trash. Especially at my supper table when we have a guest present. I have to admit that boy's name would have gagged a maggot plumb to death, but you can't be using bad language."

"I'm so sorry. Don't wash my mouth out. I promise to try harder, but you got to admit that I was right." Bodine cocked her head to one side and stared at Roxie.

"Hit the nail right on the head," Roxie said. "That's the only reason you don't have to bite off a chunk of soap and chew it up."

"Thank you. And one other thing. There ain't a guest here. Are you going to need Dee to find your walkin' cane for you? Jack ain't company. He's family."

"Girl, I'll have a sharp mind when I'm so old Methuselah will look like a teenager." Roxie shot another look down the table at Bodine.

"Thank you, Bodine," Jack said. "I'd begun to think I'd lost my place."

"Not you, Jack. We all know you're part of the family. That's why Dee can't be marrying you. It'd be incest," Bodine said.

Dee blushed scarlet. "Where did you hear that word?"

"I'm not a baby. I go to school and take health classes. They even told us about reproduction and the whole thing," Bodine announced.

"Knowing what something is and knowing when it's not appropriate to discuss it means you are growing up. Little children say things when they should be keeping their mouth shut," Tally told her.

Bodine nodded her head. "I'm sorry again. This growing up business is sure hard, ain't it?"

"Yes it is," Dee told her. "Now who's ready for dessert? I'll bring in the cake and ice cream."

Tally started to rise. "I'll help."

Jack was on his feet instantly. "No, this is your day. Today you're released from the tombs, so I'll help."

Tally raised an eyebrow to Roxie. "So?"

"It's only been a week. It'll take more time. So, no one can say a word. Not even you, Bodine," Roxie whispered.

Bodine pushed her plate back, saving both her fork and spoon. It wasn't every day that Roxie made both a banana nut cake and ice cream. "Couldn't if I wanted to. I have no idea what you are talking about."

Dee carried the pedestal cake plate with gold edging and set it on the table. A three-tiered banana cake rested on top. "Ta-da!"

Jack brought in the ice cream canister wrapped in a tea towel. "Double ta-da!"

Mimosa handed the first serving of each to Tally. "Enjoy this."

Tally scooped up ice cream on her cake, cut a piece off, and slowly put it into her mouth. "Heaven," she muttered.

"Remember how good that tastes when you get a notion to gamble again," Roxie said.

Tally gave Roxie a thumbs-up sign and kept eating.

Bodine ate as fast as she could to keep the ice cream from melting. "Do we have to stay for the sunset on the back porch, Tally? Oh, no, I've got a brain freeze."

"Well, slow down, child," Mimosa said. "The frogs have been down at Buckhorn forever. You don't have to eat so fast."

"Yes, tonight we have to stay," Tally said. "I wouldn't miss a single moment of tradition this day. After we have our lemonade, then we'll go to the lake. We can stay up late if they're biting or if the frogs are playing hide-and-go-seek."

Bodine pouted. "Oh, okay. I'm glad it's not my day to clean up."

"I'll do the cleanup after we enjoy the sunset," Dee offered.

"It's not your day either," Bodine said.

"No, but I missed my day for seven years," Dee reminded her.

"And you've got to be extra nice because you married a prissy northerner," Bodine said.

"That's right," Dee said.

"I'll help," Jack said.

"Southern men don't do dishes. They take out the trash when they aren't whining about a football game," Bodine told him seriously.

"Oops! Someone forgot to tell me that," Jack said. "So since I didn't know until after I offered to help, then I'll have to just suck it up and help, won't I?"

"That'll teach you to ask me about manners before you open your mouth," Bodine said.

Roxie made drinks, and they carried them to the porch to watch the sun set. Tradition couldn't be broken, especially not on a night when her whole family was home. Bodine sipped her second glass of lemonade and chased fireflies, then ran up to her room to change into shorts and a T-shirt, find her old fishing hat, and fuss at her mother to hurry up so they could go find her frog.

Roxie rocked lazily in her chair. The sun put on a spectacular show. Bright orange, brilliant pink, red, and every color in between. Hot summer night. Cold lemonade in a tall glass with lots of ice. Appetite sated with good southern cooking. All her girls were home. Jack was there. Heaven couldn't be one whit more glorious.

Dee and Jack finished their drinks and went back inside to clean the table and load the dishwasher. Even though it had been years since they'd shared kitchen duties, they still worked together as well as they had in junior high. He removed the serving bowls, found plastic containers to put the leftovers in. She carried the plates, glasses, and silverware to the countertop to be rinsed and put into the dishwasher.

"So what's on your agenda for the rest of this Saturday night? Got a hot date in the old town? Going to jump in that big truck and go run up and down Sulphur's Main Street?" he asked.

"I've kinda outgrown dragging Main. Haven't got a hot date. Don't really know if I'm ready for dates, hot or cold. I don't think I am. I may be an old maid. The crazy old woman in the red house out on the Buckhorn Corner. Don't go too close to her or she'll turn you into a lizard."

"Or a frog?" Jack snapped the lid on what was left of the baked beans and found a place in the refrigerator for it.

Dee looked at him. Not bad, the way he filled out those freshly starched jeans. Right fine, the way his knit shirt pulled across his firm biceps. She quickly turned back to her job before he saw her staring. "Not a frog. I wouldn't change a kid into a frog. Bodine might find it and boil it in her potion."

"Want to come over to the trailer and watch a movie? I rented a couple while I was in town. One with Richard Gere and one called *Carolina* with Julia Stiles," he said.

"I'd love to," she said. "It's been years since I spent a Saturday night watching movies."

"Good Lord, Dee, what did you do on Saturday night out there? Didn't they have VCRs or DVDs?"

"Both, but Saturday night was for socializing among the rich and shameless. Dinner parties at the country club. Small gatherings sometimes at a fancy restaurant. No popcorn and movies. No lemonade on the back porch. Every minute was used for the business."

He kissed her quickly on the cheek. "You poor undernourished darlin'."

The touch of his lips turned her cheeks scarlet.

"It was a tough business, but someone had to do it. I just hope Ray's new wife is up for the challenge." She teased to cover up the embarrassment.

"There'll be no more cussin' in Roxie's kitchen," he whispered conspiratorially. "You say that man's name again and she'll be making you eat soap."

"Yes, sir. Now that we have this job done, can I go change into shorts and a T-shirt, or is movie watching considered formal?"

"Redneck formal. No spaghetti stains on your shirt and no holes in your shorts."

"Sounds downright wonderful to me. Don't wait for me, though. Go on over to your place and get things going. I'll be there in a few minutes."

"You wouldn't stand me up now, would you?"

"Honey, I wouldn't think of it. Not with Richard Gere on the tube."

Chapter Five

Jack tried to breathe but it was barely a wheezing snort. His forehead was on fire. The rest of his body felt as if he'd been immersed in a tub of ice water. He pulled the covers tightly up around his neck and fumbled for the remote control shoved down between the couch cushions. It should be against the law to catch a cold in the summer.

Drawing the quilt tighter around his shivering body, he peeked out the window behind the sofa. She was in there. In the store, keeping shop for him while he hung on to life by a thread. Okay, okay, so it wasn't a life or death situation. It sure felt like it right at that moment. He groaned and threw himself back on the pillows. The announcer on the television told him that *Days of Our Lives* was next on the tube. Nanna's show, he remembered. She watched it faithfully. It was the fifth love of her life. Her husband being the first. Her son, second. Jack, third. Fishing, fourth. And *Days of Our Lives,* fifth.

Jack would have rather been out in the store or over at Roxie's. Not laid up with a bug that Bodine declared was the result of biological warfare waged by some little country with a name no one could pronounce. She said that they put the flu powder on the wings of buzzards and turned them loose over the United States to spread the biological warfare sickness. She'd learned about the possibility of such a thing in science class and it had instantly become proven fact. She'd promised that she'd brew a special potion and leave it on his front porch when she came home from school. He might just be tempted to drink it if he didn't feel better by then. Who cared if her brew included boiled lake frogs? He'd be the guinea pig if it was guaranteed to make him well.

"Good grief." Dee shook her head as she eyed the shelves in the store. How long had it been since Jack had given the place a good scrubbing? Sure, the bread man kept the shelves stocked with fresh goods. The snack man made sure there was lots of junk food to tempt even those campers with the greatest willpower. But there was enough dust on the shelf to grow a crop of watermelons.

Nanna always kept the place spotless in between her fishing trips. Somehow in the last seven years, the store had begun to look as if it had one foot in the grave and one on a boiled okra pod. Dee found a galvanized mop bucket in the bathroom, filled it with disinfectant and warm water, located Nanna's old scrub rags, and went to work. She popped open a paper bag with a flourish and filled it with outdated medicine, shaking her head as she tossed in Tylenol that had expired three years before.

The telephone rang as she toted a bag out to the Dumpster behind the store. She ignored it, but it kept up the incessant howling until she answered it.

"What are you throwing away?" Jack asked.

"Stuff that should have been tossed years ago. Did you know that you've got things that were old when Moses was a baby? And besides, what are you doing spying on me, Jack Brewer? You are supposed to be sleeping and getting well. Roxie is making chicken soup for you and Granny Branson. She's got the hootus too. The three B&B queens are meeting at Branson's Inn and having chicken soup and telling tales to frighten children in an attempt to make Granny Branson laugh and feel better." She held the phone against her right shoulder and wiped down the medicine display shelf. Aspirin, gauze, nose spray, allergy medicine.

"So the queens are in session?" He coughed until he sounded like he might expel a lung.

"Yes, they are, so Murray County better beware. Roxie, Molly, and Etta. Rivals at business. Best friends at heart."

"Roxie's already given it up. Molly says she's ready to retire. That just leaves Etta, and she's not in good health." Jack sneezed four times in rapid succession.

"Stop talking and go get some rest. I'll get this place cleaned and then bring you some soup for supper. Roxie's already gone to Branson's Inn. We're having Mexican chicken for supper, and if you're up to it, I'll bring a slab of that over too."

"I'm up for it, I promise. I love Roxie's Mexican chicken. Did you know that Stella married some fellow from California and last time the queens were in session, Molly said things weren't going so well." Jack was reluctant to hang up and go back to the soap opera.

"No, hadn't heard anything. What about Roseanna?" Dee asked about Etta's granddaughter. The three of them, Dee, Rosie, and Stella, had grown up together. All three had grandmothers who ran bed and breakfast establishments.

"Roseanna married a rich man from Tulsa. Some fancy man."

"Roseanna Cahill? Surely we're not talking about the same woman. She and Jodie wore jeans all the time, rode bulls, did the rodeo circuit. Tulsa?" Dee stopped cleaning for a minute to let that soak in.

"She worked on the police force as some kind of special tracking person until she ran off with Mr. Fancy Pants. Come to think of it, you did the same. Didn't ride bulls or rodeo, but ran off with Mr. Fancy Pants."

"My shoulder is cramping from holding this phone, and I don't want to hear about the past. I'm hanging up, so good-bye, Jack. Get some rest. I'll bring you soup for supper."

"Will you stay and talk to me while I eat it?"

"Of course. But only if you promise you won't pawn the flu off on me." She hung up the phone before he had time to find something else to talk about.

She rolled her head around in circles to get the kink out of her neck and went back to cleaning. By the time she had the shelves all cleaned, the glass doors of the coolers sparkling, and the floor mopped, she was sweaty and tired. She popped open a can of Dr Pepper, plopped down in the worn, old vinyl chair behind the counter and propped her feet up beside the cash register.

Ray would have been mortified if he'd seen her dressed like that, drinking from the can like a common hoyden, strands of hair escaping from the plastic headband holding it back from her face. Maybe he was right. You could take the girl from the gutter but not the gutter from the girl. He'd taken her from Buckhorn Corner, away from southern Oklahoma, and she'd survived; was a quick study in corporate wifedom. But the yearning had always been there to go back to her gutter, where she was accepted just as she was.

It was hard to think of Roseanna Cahill living in Tulsa. Jack had to be joking. She could easily see her in California. Tall. Pretty. A smile to die for. Legs that went from earth to heaven. Movie-star material for sure. But Roseanna in Tulsa? She shook her head involuntarily.

Roxie swung open the store's door, letting the screen door slam behind her. "Looks like you've put in a profitable day. Almost gives a body the shivers, though. Looks like Myrtle came back from the dead and cleaned the place."

Roxie wore a pair of her Spandex capris, lime green, with a Hawaiian-print shirt that buttoned up the front, the top two buttons left open. Hot-pink flip-flops with what she called kitten heels. She'd tied her ratted hair back with a bright yellow scarf, letting the ends hang over one shoulder. Dee needed to put on sunglasses with that much brightness but she just shaded her eyes with the back of her hand.

"It needed cleanin', and that door hasn't been opened all day until you came in. Guess most of the tourist season is over. So how were the queens?"

Roxie snapped open a folding chair and sat down beside her granddaughter. "Oh, Molly isn't doing so good. Her immune system is shot all to the devil. All that stuff they pumped in her veins to kill the cancer took its toll on her system. Every little bug that floats through the county stays with her. But she did have news of Stella. You know, it must be something in the water at the B&B businesses. All three of you girls got the short end of the stick when it came to men folk. Guess it's partially our fault. Raising you up without any men around to speak of. You didn't know the male gender could be such rascals. At least you and Stella didn't. Roseanna had a good father for a role model. Give me one of those things you're drinking. Hotter'n a back seat in hell, ain't it?"

Dee's sweaty thighs made a sucking noise as they left the vinyl chair. She tugged her shorts down and fetched a Dr Pepper, thumbing back the tab as she walked back. "Haven't got a glass. So you'll have to lower your standards and drink from the can. So what's the news on Stella?"

"It's so hot, I'd almost drink it from the potty. Stella's news is that she's unhappy. Man is a regular horse's hind end. Stella can't do squat right, and yet she stays with him. Molly says she's left the door open for her to come home any time she wants. She married that boy just older than you all. Mitch, who was too pretty for a boy and thought he was movie-star material. He's out there in California letting Stella support him while he runs around looking for a movie to star in. Worthless is what he is." Roxie sipped at the cold soda pop.

"And he's not even a Yankee," Dee grinned.

"Men are men. Yankees are just worse than the average lot. Besides, Roseanna almost married one."

"Almost?" Dee blew a hair away from her mouth. She picked up the fly swatter from beside the cash register and flattened two varmints before she turned her Dr Pepper up again, trying in vain to cool off from the inside out.

"They're living in Tulsa but that man of hers grew up in California. That's not the north, but it's just as bad. They live in the penthouse in some big fancy place. Ain't no way Roseanna is going to get up in the morning, put on her boots, and go for a horseback ride to check on the cattle before breakfast, now is there?" Roxie mopped her brow with a paper towel she took off the roller beside the cash register.

"Guess there might be something in the water here to make us go through a stupid phase. I'm just glad mine is over."

"Is it?"

"I'm here, ain't I?" Dee snapped. "I'm sorry. I shouldn't have spoken like that."

"Accepted. But you aren't through your stupid phase yet, sugar. Not until you wake up and smell the coffee brewing right under your nose."

"You mean Jack, don't you? Roxie, we're the best of friends. Why would I ruin that for a husband?"

"The best relationships in the world come with friendship and passion combined. I'm going home to where there's enough air-conditioning to harden up my fat cells. They're about to all melt away in this place. Why Jack don't put in air-conditioning is beyond me. Sit here in this heat all day. It's a sin."

"He likes it, evidently. Goodness knows it's not because he can't afford it."

"Most likely it's because he don't want the customers to stay very long." Roxie patted Dee on the shoulder.

She'd only been gone a few minutes when two young men slipped in the door. They went to the cooler, took out two suitcases of beer, set them on the counter along with two big bags of corn chips and a can of bean dip. Dee could have shouted. The day wasn't going to be a complete bust. She'd at least have more than the hundred dollars of start-up money in the till when the day was finished.

"I'll need some ID." She eyed the two men carefully.

If either of them was a day over sixteen she'd be surprised, so there went the price of beer. All she would have in the till would be the price of two bags of chips and a can of bean dip. At least it would beat nothing.

"Sure, lady, we got ID. The most important kind." One of them pointed a pistol at her heart. "Now you empty what's in that cash drawer and we'll take it right along with this little bit of refreshment. Then I think we'll take you to the back room. Tie you up so you won't be calling the law on us."

"Boys, you don't want to do this." She was amazed that words came from her dry mouth.

Nanna had told her for years she'd never go to the back room if robbers came into the store. If they were going to kill her, they'd have to do it right in front of the glass windows where God and everyone else could see. "Just put that gun away and walk on out of here."

"I don't think so," the other one chuckled. "I think we're having the money, the beer, and the woman."

Roxie slung open the screen door and pointed a double-barreled shotgun at their backs. "Well, I think different. Now you both best turn around right easy and put that gun on the floor. Dee, you step on over to the side. I wouldn't want to get blood on you if I have to pull these triggers."

"You're just an old woman. You wouldn't have the guts to shoot us." The one with the gun spun around and pointed the pistol at her.

She cocked the hammer back and sighted down the barrel, not blinking or flinching. She stepped around closer to Dee but kept the gun trained on the biggest of the boys. "That, young man, is where you're wrong.

You wouldn't be the first young punk who's bled on this floor. The last one is providin' fertilizer for the rose-bushes out back. Didn't even call the sheriff or his family. Just plugged him and planted him."

"Put the gun down, man. She ain't bluffin'. She's crazy. You can see it in her eyes," the smaller of the two said.

"Call the police, Dee," Roxie said calmly.

"Run!" The one with the gun yelled and took off out the door so fast the other one had to think fast to get enough traction to even follow in his wake.

Roxie stepped to the door and fired one round right over their heads, giggling when the one with the gun did a little fancy step dance right before he bailed into the driver's seat of a low-slung convertible. She fired another round as the second one ran alongside the car, holding onto the door handle and trying to get inside the moving vehicle at the same time. The boom seemed to put a little fire into his efforts. He let out a wailing scream and bounded into the passenger's seat, slamming the door behind him.

"Roxie! What have you done?" Dee shouted.

Roxie lowered the gun and pointed her finger at Dee. "Don't you raise your voice to me. I didn't hit them. They'll be searching over their skinny little hind ends looking to see if they're bleeding, but they aren't. If I'd wanted them filled with holes, they would be. I just wanted to scare the devil out of them. Now give me that cordless phone."

Dee gave it to her with trembling hands.

Roxie poked in the numbers without even a twitch. "Sheriff, this is Roxie Hooper. Couple of young Texans just tried to rob the store out here at Buckhorn Corner. I shot in the air to scare them right good, and they're probably still shakin' in their boxers. They're armed with one of those fancy new pistols that looks like the cops use on the television shows. I think it's called a Glock. And they're driving a brand-new little Thunderbird convertible. Red. With a license plate that reads STUD89. Headed right into the park. Left here two minutes ago. Just thought you'd like to know. Sure thing, Sheriff. I'll just come on in right now. That way it'll be done before suppertime. Want me to bring you a quart of chicken soup? Jack and Molly are both ailin', so I made it today."

Roxie listened for a while and then nodded. "Lock it up, Dee. We got to go identify us a couple of petrified little boys."

"I need to call Jack. I can't go anywhere lookin' like this, Roxie. Can I have ten minutes to shower and change?"

"I'll call Jack. You dash on over to the house and get changed. By the time I get the soup in the jar, you be back downstairs. They'll have those baby boys in the jail by the time we get there."

Dee was already opening the front door. "How do you know that?"

"Because the dispatcher put it out on the air while I was talking to the sheriff and the car was already in the park. They're following it now. By the time we get to the jail, they'll be waiting—whining and screaming about me shootin' at them." Roxie dialed the familiar number of the trailer behind the store.

It was the quickest shower Dee ever had. She jerked a pair of khaki walking shorts over her half-dried body, a turquoise T-shirt over her head, and her feet into a pair of sandals. By the time she was downstairs, Roxie came out of the kitchen toting a jar of chicken soup and half a loaf of fresh bread. Before either of them reached the front door, it swung open and Jack rushed in, combing back his wet hair with his fingertips.

"What are you doing up?" Roxie asked.

"I'm going with you. Are you all right, Dee? They didn't hurt you, did they?" He eyed her up and down, making sure Roxie hadn't told a lie when she assured him over and over that the robbers hadn't laid a hand on Dee.

"No, they didn't hurt me. But I have to admit, looking down the barrel of that mean-looking gun did give me the jitters. Sheriff just called, though, and they've already got them behind bars. We're just going down there to sign the papers that they're actually the ones who attempted armed robbery."

Jack knew her well enough to hear the slight difference in her voice. "I'm going to drive you. Come on."

"But you are sick," Roxie argued.

"I was. This scared the flu right out of me."

"Hmmph," Roxie snorted. "If I'd known that would work, I wouldn't have spent the day boiling chickens."

"You sure you're all right?" Jack asked as they paraded out to Roxie's Caddy.

"I'm fine, honest. It all happened so fast. First they were there, then Roxie pointing that shotgun."

"And a good thing," Roxie said from the driver's seat. "I was standing on my front porch when I noticed those two getting out of that little low-slung sportscar. Seemed too young to own something that expensive, and then the one reached into the back seat and put on a jacket. Now, there is definitely something wrong with a person who'd wear a jacket in this kind of heat. About that time he stuffed that gun down in his pocket, and the two of them high-fived each other. That's when I knew there was something going on, and Dee didn't even know where your grandpa kept that blunderbuss under the counter. So I just grabbed the old shotgun and beat a path right back over there."

"And I'm glad you did." Dee shivered.

Sheriff Mitchum nodded when they walked into his office. "Afternoon, Roxie, Dee, and Jack. We got 'em. One in each interrogatin' room. Car was stolen yesterday in Sherman, Texas. Gun was taken from a pawn shop in Gainesville this morning. They hit a convenience store in Durant at noon and one in Dickson just before they stopped by your place. Neither one of them is talkin' yet and neither one of them has a driver's license. Fifteen years old. What's the world comin' to?"

"Called their parents yet?" Roxie asked.

"Yes, they're on their way up here from Sherman. It's not the first time they've been in trouble with the law. Don't expect it will be the last. You want to identify them for positive, Dee? You too, Roxie? The driver says this crazy old woman just opened up fire on them when they didn't have enough cash to pay for their beer."

"They called Roxie old and crazy?" Jack stifled a roar.

"They sure did." The sheriff nodded. "Follow me and we'll get this over with. We'll turn them over to the juvenile authorities when their parents get here. Funny thing, these boys will have to contend with the juvies, but they'll have closed, clear records when they're eighteen. If they'd been adults, they would have done hard time for this."

"That's the woman! That's the crazy old witch who shot at me," the young boy said when the sheriff threw open the door, letting Roxie and Dee enter the room ahead of him.

"And this is the young ignorant fool who tried to rob the store." Roxie placed both hands on the table and looked the boy right in the eye.

"He held a gun on me and threatened to physically harm me," Dee said. "He's the one who had the gun. The other one wasn't nearly as cocky."

"They're both lying," the boy said. "We didn't have a gun in the store at all. We just didn't have enough money to pay for the beer, and she got all huffy and mad about it. Then that old broad tried to kill us both."

Roxie leaned in and whispered. "Honey, you tell it any way you please, but we both know what happened in that store. And you'd better know that if I'd wanted you dead you would be pushin' up tomato plants in my garden. I shot above your heads to scare you, and it worked. If I'd wanted to shoot the elastic out of your cute little jeans you got ridin' down on your hips, I could have done that and never even messed up those sweet little checkered boxer shorts. One other thing, I'm not old and I'm not crazy, not yet, but I might get that way so if I was you, I'd steer clear of Buckhorn Corner."

"She's threatening me. What are you going to do about that, Sheriff?" the kid whined.

"I'd say she's statin' facts, child. Roxie, if y'all will come with me, we'll ID the other suspect. Oh, you'll be having a few other visitors before dark when we put you in a cell." He turned back to the boy. "Couple of other places you robbed are sending their clerks up here for ID, and your neighbor whose car you stole, and then there's the pawnshop owner. I expect they're all out to get you too."

The kid slammed his head down into his hands without answering.

"Lord, save me from boy kids." Roxie shook her head in dismay. "I'm glad the pups I had to raise were at least girl kids."

Jack slipped his arm around Dee's shoulders and drew her close. "I'm so so sorry. I'll never leave you in the store alone again."

"Oh, hush. You couldn't have known. You didn't plan on getting sick and being robbed the same day."

Jack hugged her tighter, trying to erase the tension in her muscles with his touch. Little did he know that it wasn't the stress of the day that caused most of the tightness in her shoulders or the high pitch to her voice, but the way she felt when he touched her. The breathless feeling she thought she'd never feel again. The emotions tearing at her heart as she fought desperately against them. She wouldn't let herself rebound into Jack's arms. She would fight against it with every ounce of willpower she had, because it would destroy their friendship when the end came. And the end would come. A year. Two years. Seven years. Take a look at Mimosa with all her failed marriages. At Tally. At Granny Branson who'd kicked out her philandering husband years and years ago. At her own experience with Ray. And even Roseanna Cahill's and Stella Branson's marriages were on the rocks. Statistics were getting them all.

Dee might have a good marriage, a wonderful one with Jack, just like Roxie had had with Henry Clay Hooper. But it was a chance she wasn't going to take. She simply was not going to let herself fall in love with her best friend.

Chapter Six

Bodine huffed as she sat on the back porch with the rest of the family and Jack while they watched the sun set. Tonight she'd put away her costumes and dressed in khaki capris and an electric-blue T-shirt that matched her eyes. "Well, I don't think it is one bit fair. I had to go sit at a school desk with yucky boys all around me and you get almost robbed. My life is boredom and yours is Hollywood."

"Thank God you were in school." Tally shuddered to think of her loquacious daughter bursting in on a near robbery. "If it had been you walking in on that robbery, those crazy boys would have shot you just to shut you up."

Bodine eyed her grandmother. "I wouldn't have missed if I'd had the shotgun. I wouldn't have needed a gun anyway. I could have thrown some of my potion on them. The one that turns them into a quivering mass of jelly when it hits their eyes."

Roxie pointed at Bodine. "And I didn't miss either, Miss Smarty Pants. I wasn't aiming to shoot either of them, just scare them and make them think twice before they come back to Buckhorn Corner with ideas of robbery."

"Well, I'm glad to hear it. I was afraid you were getting old." Bodine smiled impishly.

Mimosa flipped her blond hair over her shoulder and cocked an ear toward the end of the house. "Wonder who that is? You expecting company, Tally?"

"No, ma'am. Wish I could say I was. Wish it would be that good-looking professor who teaches my government class. The way he fills out those blue jeans just about gives me a case of the vapors. And boots. I'm a pure sucker for a man in cowboy boots and tight-fittin' jeans." Tally all but swooned.

"You got a new addiction?" Mimosa asked.

"At least it's a healthy, normal one, and it doesn't have a thing to do with a slot machine or a lottery ticket. Don't sound big enough to be a truck coming to carry you back on the road." Roxie shot Mimosa a look.

"I told you, I'm retired. I'm going to be a beautician. Set up shop right in Sulphur and bring home all the gossip every night to tell y'all when we sit on the porch after supper," Mimosa said seriously.

The sound of a car door slamming echoed through the still evening air. "Guess we'll know in a little while, won't we? Bet it's Miz Etta. She's not been around in a while for a visit." Bodine speculated, but no one got up.

If it were a stranger, they'd hear the doorbell. If it were a friend, they'd know where Roxie was by the setting of the sun. Some things never changed, and Roxie's evening habit of watching the sun set was more predictable than whether the sun would come up in the east and set in the west every day.

The doorbell rang. Bodine hopped up and ran in the back door, and through the kitchen, the dining room, and the living room to the front door. She threw it open to indeed find a strange man standing there, a briefcase in one hand, wearing a three-piece black suit.

"You sellin' something or talkin' religion?"

"Neither. I'd like to talk to Dee," he said.

"Well, she ain't interested in buyin' nothing in that briefcase or listenin' to you give a sermon neither, and I don't believe you, Mister. Any fool who'd wear a getup like that on a hot day like this is thinks he's going to save the world, and we ain't in no mood for a come-to-Jesus talk tonight."

"I'm Ray, her ex-husband, and I would like to speak to Dee, little girl. Now you go get her."

Bodine raised her chin. "Don't you take that tone with me. I could turn you into a frog in a second. I am a witch on some days. It's just that today I'm a common girl. But I could be a witch in the length of time it takes me to go put on my getup, so you better mind your manners. I guess those who were in the war of northern aggression don't think they have to be polite and say please and thank you. So now what's the magic word, Mister Ray?"

"The magic word is *now*. I said go get Dee . . . now!" He would like to strangle that child. Hopefully his and Angie's daughter wouldn't be a sassy kid like this one.

Bodine slammed the door in his face and retraced her footsteps to the back porch where she plopped down on the steps with her usual overstated drama.

"Who was it?" Tally pushed a lock of blond hair back behind her ear and set her empty glass on the table between her and Roxie.

Bodine put one hand on her forehead. "Some fool selling religion. I told him we were all nuns and unless he wanted to make a donation to our convent, The Mercy of the Red House, then we weren't interested in his sermon. Oh, dear, it is a hot evening, isn't it? Do you think Rhett Butler will be coming around the house to see me before that hot sun sets?"

They all laughed with her.

"Honey, you must have decided to be Miss Scarlett instead of a common girl after all. You think you need to go get into costume to make it official?" Roxie asked.

"No, ma'am. I do declare, Dee, if it ain't the devil himself coming around the end of the house. You watch out now, sugar, that man is plumb rude. Wouldn't say please or thank you, so I just slammed the door right in his face," Bodine said in her best Scarlett O'Hara voice and nodded toward Ray, picking his way around the flower beds toward the porch.

"Dee?" He looked up to see four women, the rude child, and a man on the back porch.

"Ray, what are you doing here?" Dee asked.

She waited for the flutters to take up residence in her stomach. To feel like a band of gypsies were dancing around a hot bonfire, turning her insides to a heated furnace, her face into a permanent blush, her mind into mush. None of it happened.

"I need to talk with you. In private. Could we go inside, or would you rather talk in my rental car?"

Jack suppressed a groan. There was Ray. Seven years older and dressed in a custom-made Italian suit. The smell of money all over him. Confidence oozing out every pore. He'd come back to tell Dee he'd made a colossal mistake and wanted her back. How could she refuse? Nothing on Buckhorn Corner could compete with what stood before her.

"I'm not going anywhere with you. Not to the car. Not inside the house. You'll remember Roxie, I'm sure. This is my mother, Mimosa. My sister, Tally. My niece, Bodine. And this is my best friend, Jack. Whatever you have to say, you can say before these folks or you can march yourself right back around the house and go home," Dee said.

Jack nodded toward the man he'd like beat to death with that eel briefcase and feed his flesh and bones to the catfish at Buckhorn Creek. They'd feast well on something that juicy.

"What I have to say involves you and me, and I'll do it in private," Ray said.

"Then good-bye, Ray. There is no you and me, and you are on my turf now. Speak or leave. It's all the same to me."

"Besides, you are not welcome in my house. Haven't been since the night you hit Dee," Roxie said. "So that leaves the car to do your dirty business in, and Dee said she's not going there. Guess it's time for you to go."

Ray set his jaw in a firm line, the muscles right under his ears doing a little tap dance. "All right then, have it your way."

No one else saw it but Dee. Just that small gesture brought her joy. She'd made him as angry as he had made her when he told her their marriage had been dissolved.

"So what is it that's so important you've come all the way to Oklahoma to see me? Are we really still married and you need me to sign papers so your precious child won't be illegitimate?"

"No, that part of our life is over. Father took care of it so that Angie and I could be married quite legally and within the church. What happened is that Aunt Marjorie died." He set his briefcase on the porch and snapped it open.

Dee paled. "Oh, no. When?"

"About a week after you left," he said with no emotion.

Dee's eyes filled with tears. "Why didn't you call me? She was my friend. The only one in your family who didn't think I was a backwoods hillbilly. I loved her. You knew that, Ray. You didn't call me on purpose."

"Why should I? You weren't part of the family anymore. If you'd come back to the funeral, it would have upset Angie." He rifled through a sheaf of papers.

Dee glared at him in disgust.

"Before she died, unbeknownst to Father or me, she changed her will. She didn't have much after the last two years in the private, very expensive nursing home where we put her when she broke her hip, but what little she did have, she's left to you. It's mostly a few pieces of cheap jewelry. I've come for your signature on these papers. Green tabs everywhere you need to sign."

She took the pen he held out. "Why did you bring them?"

"We thought it best. Father and I did."

A wind of ill bode swept over Dee. All she had to do was sign the papers and then the little that Aunt Marjorie had left would be hers. Bless the woman's heart. She'd only produced one son, and he'd been killed in Vietnam. She and Ray's father had been the sole heirs of the company when their own parents died. But evidently her share had been used up. Dee was numb from the shock of knowing Aunt Marjorie was actually gone. She'd been the only person she felt a need to tell good-bye when she left the state more than three months before. Aunt Marjorie had been sitting in her wheelchair, makeup on, hair fixed in the latest style, dressed in an expensive suit, her mind as sharp as it had been when she was a young woman.

"Just sign it," Ray said impatiently.

"No, I don't think so. Not until I have my lawyer look at it. I don't think you are being honest with me."

Ray smiled slyly. "It's just a simple will, Dee. All you need to do is sign it. You don't have to pay a lawyer to read it for you. That's just money wasted. Our marriage didn't work, but I'd be honest with you. Don't you believe me?"

"I don't think I do. So why don't you just leave and my lawyer will look at these papers and get back to you? Now unless you've got some other lies to tell me, you'd better be going." Her tone lacked warmth and trust.

Ray clenched his teeth. The plan had failed. Even a backwoods lawyer could understand what was in those papers. Angie was going to pitch a fit when she heard that Dee had the option of sitting in on every business meeting the company had. That she had enough stock to vote or veto every motion he made. Most of all, that Angie wouldn't be getting that million dollars' worth of jewelry locked up in the lawyer's vault. She'd already planned to wear the rubies to the Christmas party.

"This is ridiculous, Dee. Sign the papers."

"I don't think so. I'll tell my lawyer to call David Zenowski tomorrow evening. He is still the in-house attorney for the company, isn't he? Is he the one who told you Aunt Marjorie had made the will solid?"

"Yes, David is handling the will. Aunt Marjorie used a different lawyer, though, or we would have taken care of it before she died."

Roxie pointed toward the end of the house. "I'm sure you would have. Now, I've been a patient woman, letting you stand there and state your case without getting my shotgun out for the second time today. But my patience has run plumb out, so get out of here. No more words. No more anything. Dee's lawyers will be in touch. Go and good riddance. You are ruining my sunset. I don't allow anything or anyone to ruin my sunsets, most especially someone I don't like."

"Told you we wasn't buyin' nothing you had to sell," Bodine told him.

Ray knew he'd been beaten, but he hadn't lost the war just yet. There was one way to get her to sign those papers, and what Angie didn't know certainly wouldn't hurt her. He'd do anything to keep his wife happy, keep on his father's good side, keep his inheritance intact.

"Good-bye," he said with a curt smile. The night was still young and his plane didn't fly out of Dallas until noon the next day. Ray could do a lot in that length of time. And enjoy the doing.

"So that's the sorry scoundrel that ruined the family's good name," Bodine said when they heard the car back out of the gravel driveway.

"No, that's just one in a long line of many. If we were talking the first one, we'd have to ask Mimosa about it, and I'm afraid her memory wouldn't stretch that far," Roxie said.

"Let's not put me in the glass case tonight," Mimosa said. "Let me see those papers, Dee. I'm not a lawyer, but I can read."

Dee shook her head and picked them up like she was handling a rattlesnake. "I'll read them first. Actually, it's written in fairly easy language." She read for a while, then looked up.

"Not much lawyer jargon at all. Just says that I'm sane, which would be stretching the truth a bit coming from this family, and that I'm relinquishing all rights to the inheritance left to me in July of this year by one Marjorie Suddeth Lancaster. It doesn't even state or list the inheritance. Could be Ray is right and it amounts to very little, but the money isn't the issue here. It's the fact that he lied and came all the way out here himself. This isn't an acceptance paper, it is a relinquishing paper. I smell a rat."

"Hmmph," Bodine snorted dramatically. "That ain't no rat you smell. It's the stink of a sorry rascal. I'd call him something worse, but Roxie would make me eat soap."

Mimosa patted her granddaughter's arm. "Well done, Bodine. I'm proud of you. You are beginning to learn your lessons. I'd never met the ex-husband, you know. He is a right fetching man. I can see where he would sweep a woman off her feet. Matter of fact, if he'd been driving an eighteen-wheeler, I might have gone pantin' after him like a hound dog after a coon myself when I was younger."

"Mimosa!" Bodine and Tally both said at the same time.

"Just statin' facts, darlin's. Just statin' facts," Mimosa said.

"Well, I reckon if Lucifer walked around the side of the house, he'd come disguised as a good-lookin' man too," Roxie said. "But it wouldn't make him an angel, no matter how much he tried."

"If he had on tight-fittin' jeans and boots, I might be so inclined to do a little pantin' myself," Tally said.

Jack leaned in closer to Dee to peer over her shoulder and read the papers with her. "It's not a will at all? It's a relinquishing of rights?"

His warm breath on her neck made a mountain of goosebumps creep up her arms and backbone. Ray, at six foot four, was several inches taller than Jack. Ray, with his jet-black hair and brooding brown eyes: movie-star qualities that would make a nun's pantyhose itch to crawl down around her ankles. Jack, with his unruly, sandy-brown hair that always needed a cut or comb, hazel eyes that glittered when he was happy and brooded when he was sad. Of the two, at first glance Ray would win the handsome-man contest. Yet he'd left her with a bitter taste in her mouth. And Jack? Well, Jack was still sitting there and she'd trust him with her very life.

"Know a good lawyer?" she asked.

"Sure. Got one I use all the time right in Sulphur. She's handled all my affairs except my mafia business." He winked at Bodine.

"Mamie Rockford?" Dee asked.

"That's the one. I'll call her when I get home this evening and see if she's going to be in the office tomorrow. I see there's a lawyer's number on the letterhead. Reckon that's who she'll need to talk to about this inheritance?"

"Yes, that's the one," Dee said. "And I want to thank all of you for closing ranks and standing with me while he was here. Thanks, Roxie, for not killing him. He's not worth the bullet. Thanks to everyone for letting me handle it the best way I could when I know you'd have liked to have done him bodily harm."

"Jack, too?" Bodine asked.

"Especially Jack. When he slipped his arm over the back of my chair, it gave me strength to tell Ray to leave." Dee looked over at her friend, who was blushing scarlet.

"Ah, 'twasn't nothing. Just didn't want you to think we weren't here for you," Jack drawled. So she'd had to have strength to tell the man to leave, had she? Did that bode well for him or against him, he wondered? If Ray ever caught her out alone without family to steady her up, would she capitulate?

"Enough of this unpleasant business. When trouble comes, it does come in threes, doesn't it?" Roxie said. "First the robbery and now this."

"That's only two. Where's the third?" Bodine asked.

"Oh, it's there. I expect Tally is thinking about gamblin' and Mimosa is thinkin' about truck drivers," Roxie said.

"I am not. I was thinking about tight-fittin' jeans and boots and a man with blue eyes." Tally defended herself.

"And I was thinkin' about cutting your hair tomorrow evening." Mimosa did the same.

"Sure you were. And I'm going to choose to believe you and hope that in this instance trouble doesn't come in threes. Now, Dee, you take Jack on home and see to it he's got Vick's rubbed on his chest and feet. Put a warm washcloth on his chest and good thick socks on his feet.

You can watch a movie with him so he won't be so lonesome, but don't keep him up late. The chicken soup won't do him a bit of good without his rest."

"Yes, ma'am," Jack said.

Dee handed Roxie the papers. "I'm not getting that awful-smelling stuff on my hands. He can put it on himself. He's not a baby."

Roxie pushed her ratted red hair back out of her face. "All men are babies when they're sick. Now get on out of here, you two. At least there won't be a young'un for me to raise if you stink."

"Roxie!" Dee blushed.

"Truth is truth. Ain't no use in sugarcoatin' it," Roxie said flippantly and carried the papers into the house.

"Shall we?" Jack offered her his arm, and the two of them disappeared across the lawns as the sun slipped beneath the horizon, twilight gone, darkness covering Buckhorn Corner one more time.

"Jack, I really do thank you for being there beside me," she said.

He opened the door and let her enter the trailer before him. "Couldn't very well get up and leave you. Sun wasn't quite down past the horizon yet. Roxie would have had my hide if I'd left before a beautiful sunset finished putting on its show."

"All teasing aside." She turned abruptly and found herself chest to chest with him, his eyes going all soft as he looked down at her upturned face.

"All teasing aside," he repeated her words in a hoarse voice.

The silhouetted tableau, lit up by on the moon, hanging like a great white light in a dark blue velvet sky twinkling with diamonds, lasted only a few seconds, but it was an eternity before he looked away and found the light switch.

She hurried to the kitchen. Away from Jack and those soft, green eyes. The moment, born because of a difficult time, had passed, but not without tossing out unwanted emotions to rattle around in her heart. "Where is the Vick's? Still keep it where Nanna always did?"

He picked up the remote and channel surfed to see what was on television. "Still in the same place, but I'm not putting it on until bedtime. No way am I wearing socks as hot as it is. Not until I have to. Then I'll turn the air-conditioning down to a notch above freezing so I won't fry."

He kept his eyes on the television, trying to make sense out of what had just happened. He'd almost kissed Dee. Was he ready for that step past friendship? He'd thought he was, but now he didn't know. What if their relationship didn't work? What if they split up too? He'd lose the best friend he ever had.

She came back into the living room and eased down in the recliner, away from the sofa where he was sprawled out, his legs stretched out over one arm, his head resting on a pillow tossed on the other end. "Well, I don't like to smell the stuff so I'm not going to argue with you."

"What do you want to watch? Looks like *Sweet Home Alabama* is playing on HBO. There're old reruns of *Law and Order*, and *Friends*," he said without looking at her.

"The movie. I wanted to see it when it came out, but going to the movies is so bohemian. Unless it's one of those you are invited to attend a premiere for."

He jerked his head around to see if she was joking. "For real. You went to premieres?"

"Of course. The governor of the great state of Oklahoma was right behind me, and Elvis Presley's ghost in front of me. Ray might be rich as Midas, but he's a great big fish in a little bitty pond. He wouldn't have taken this southern rebel to a premiere even if he'd been invited."

"What are you going to do with what his aunt left you?" Jack changed the subject as he poked the buttons to bring up the movie, which was just beginning.

"Depends on how much there is. I reckon it's a sight more than he wanted to tell me about since he came down here himself and since he mentioned they'd tried to break the will. The jewelry? Well, honey, it's not going to be handed back to him for Angie to wear. If she wants rubies, and Aunt Marjorie was real partial to a mixture of diamonds and rubies, then Ray can buy them for her," she said.

"Little touch of bitterness there?"

"Probably, but I'm entitled," she snapped.

"That mean you still got feelings for the man?" Jack didn't look at her when he asked.

"I'm not going to answer that question. I'm going to watch this movie and pretend you didn't even ask it."

In an hour and a half, the movie had raised more questions than she wanted to face. Had she always loved Jack as more than a friend and had hoped down deep inside her soul that he would still be single when she came home to Oklahoma? Where did Ray fit? Was Jack right in thinking she still had feelings for the man? After all, they'd spent seven years together. Could she turn her feelings off and on like a water faucet?

"So?" Jack asked when the end credit rolled.

"So what?" she asked right back.

"Did you like it?"

"Loved it. I want to own it and watch it every week."

"Which one is Ray? The husband or the fiancé?" He picked a fight. Maybe it was because she'd said what she did about needing the strength of family and one old friend to help her reject the Yank.

"Neither," she raised her voice.

"Hey, don't holler at me. I'm just asking the question you need to answer before you can get on with your life, darlin'."

"You're being obnoxious." She stormed out the door, slamming it behind her.

God save her from men. The Big Man Upstairs had surely known what he was doing when he made all the Hooper women. If she'd have had a brother, she would have considered going home and strangling him in his sleep right then. Ray was a first-rate skunk. Jack was a meddling rascal.

She stomped across the yard and into the house. "Don't say a word to me. I'm going to bed, and I don't want to hear about Ray or Jack or which one is a husband and which one is a fiancé or a friend," she told

Roxie, Tally, Mimosa, and Bodine, who were finishing a game of Scrabble at the dining-room table.

"Whew, sounds like she and Jack just had a big one." Tally fanned her face with her hand.

"Who won?" Bodine asked.

"No tellin'," Roxie said. "I'd say it's still up in the air from the way she's acting."

"It's a good sign." Mimosa added up the points while Bodine put the game away.

"How's that?" Tally asked.

"It was going too easy. They've been kind of sitting on a blanket, falling in love without realizing it the past few weeks. They need some conflict. Some kind of big old fight to see if they'd survive in the real world of relationships."

"Well, I do declare, my mother is a philosophizer," Tally laughed.

"No, just statin' facts. Folks who have everything all perfect and then marry are in for a rude awakening."

"Voice of experience?" Roxie asked.

"Third husband. Perfect. Cards. Roses. Love oozing out of him. First time we had a disagreement, it rocked the marriage so bad it never was right again. Remember that which does not kill us makes us stronger."

"Think it'll kill them?" Tally asked.

"No, I think it'll make them stronger," Mimosa said. "Now, Bodine Delight Hooper, it is your bedtime. So go say your prayers and get to sleep. You little minx, you've whipped us all at Scrabble. When did you get so smart?"

"I was born that way." Bodine ran up the stairs before her grandmother could swat her bottom.

Dee jerked off her T-shirt and slammed it on the floor, angry that it didn't make any noise. She unzipped her shorts and flung them against the wall. Still no noise. She had a lamp in her hand and was about to hurl it at the door when she realized what she was doing. Roxie would go into an instant heart attack if Dee shattered an antique. She carefully put it back on the nightstand and instead chucked her shoes at the door. At least that brought a little instant gratification.

When she'd showered and flung herself onto the bed, with a good-sized mad still storming through her, she laced her fingers behind her head and stared at the darkened ceiling. She'd thought she was over the hissy-fit stage, even past the numb stage and moving on with her life.

You are, crazy woman. You couldn't care less about Ray. He didn't set your heart to fluttering or put you in a black mood. It's Jack you're angry with, girl. You're mad because you can't control the way you feel and because it scares the devil out of you.

Chapter Seven

Jack slam-dunked his pillow on the floor. As a child, he hated it when he and Dee argued. As an adult, it was ten times worse. It was his fault, pressuring her like that because of what she'd said about needing strength to say no to Ray. He picked up the newest John Sandford mystery and read ten pages before he realized he was looking at words and hadn't retained a single idea from the book.

He looked out the front window across the lawn at the big house next door. Lights were on upstairs, but the downstairs was dark. When they were kids, if he remembered something after Dee went to sleep, he'd throw gravel at her window and she'd open it and lean out to see what he wanted. He wondered if she was sleeping yet.

He slipped his feet back into his rubber flip-flops and was almost at the house when the lights in her bedroom window went out. He picked up a handful of gravel, then changed his mind. Perhaps they'd do better to sleep on the argument. It might not seem so big by morning, and by then they could even find humor in it. He dropped the gravel and went to the front porch. Easing himself down into the swing at the far end of the porch, he started a rhythmic motion, back and forth, with his foot. Someday he was going to build a deck on the back of the trailer and install some kind of swing. A man could solve all the problems of the world sitting in a porch swing with the late summer-night breezes cooling down the daytime temperatures.

Dee squeezed her eyes shut, but sleep wouldn't come. All she could see was Ray in that expensive suit, barely a bead of sweat on him even though the outside temperature was near a hundred degrees. Like some kind of Italian mafia don, telling her to sign her name to the papers without reading them. Just as he'd always been, from day one of their marriage: he spoke, she obeyed.

Resentment, bitterness, anger—all balled into one big round lump that was difficult to swallow. She might have forgiven him for an affair with Angie, or would she? Had she wanted a normal family so badly that she would have stood on the sidelines of an affair and taken him back?

Sure, she'd been discontent with the way she'd been raised. What kid wasn't? But she'd been jealous of those who had a traditional mother who came to school parties in plain old jeans and T-shirts, who came toting uneven cupcakes with thick icing. Hell's bells, she even called her mother by her given name—Mimosa. Then there was Roxie, who had brought perfect petit fours with little flowers on the tops to all of her school functions. Who wore ruffles, ruffles, and more ruffles, ratted hair, and three-inch heels.

She remembered the first fight she got into at school. Lisa Colley asked if her grandmother was a madam. Dee had told her that Roxie was just a grandma, that's all, but that she called her Roxie because that's the way they did things in the Hooper house. But after she'd asked Tally what a madam was, Lisa Colley was taken home the next day with a black eye and a bloody nose. Dee had spent every recess in detention for two weeks and figured it was time well spent.

She smiled thinking about that day, but a frown replaced it before it had time to really blossom. Somewhere deep inside her heart, she thought she'd find a normal happy home with Ray. What she'd landed in was as dysfunctional as what she'd jumped out of. *From the fryin' pan straight into the fire,* it seemed as if Roxie's voice whispered over her shoulder. She jerked her head around, half expecting to see her grandmother standing beside the bed.

She'd been so angry at Ray, so numb with the knowledge of what a fool she'd been, that she hadn't had time to think about what would happen if she ever had to face him again. Well, she'd faced him all right, and instead of wanting to beg him to take her back and she'd forgive him, she'd wanted to do just what Bodine had

suggested earlier. Shoot him and bury him. Was it under the compost pile? Or in the basement? No, the
basement was Jack's idea.

Jack! Oh, no! She'd been so hateful to him. But then,
he'd been just as obnoxious, thinking she was still har-
boring feelings for a man who'd been willing to cut her
heart out with a dull butter knife, throw it on the floor,
and stomp it with his imported shoes until it stopped
beating. No, she didn't have any feelings for Ray anymore. But she shouldn't have to tell Jack that. She
shouldn't have to explain a thing to him. He was her very
best friend. He should know without asking. He should
see with his eyes shut. Hear with his ears plugged with
cotton. Jack knew her better than anyone in the world.
Why was he so pushy about hearing her say the words?

Her eyes grew heavy. She wrapped her arms around
the extra pillow and snuggled. Tomorrow she'd tell him
if it was so important for him to hear the words in his
own little ears. See the expression on her face. Know
without faith. Tomorrow she'd make the argument go
away. Right now she was going to sleep.

The steady, quiet motion of the swing and Jack's own
thoughts had practically put him to sleep when he heard
the distinct crunch of gravel under someone's feet. He
set his heel down on the porch without making a sound
and watched the dark shadow of someone sneaking up
to the front porch. Ray fumbled around under the little
ceramic frog in the middle of the cast-iron table, giving
a snort when he found the spare key.

Red-hot rage plowed its way from Jack's mind to his heart, down to the pits of his stomach. As far back as he could remember, that frog had held the spare key, but how did Ray know that? Unless Dee had had second thoughts and called him. He'd just bet the man carried a cell phone with him, and he'd bet even more that he still had the same number he'd had when he and Dee were married. She'd called him and told him where to find the key, to come to her room quietly, and they'd talk again about the papers.

Well, if that's the way she wanted things, then she could have them that way. He scooted his feet around until he found his flip-flops and, wearing them on the wrong feet, he started down the front steps to the yard.

Whoa, buddy boy. So what makes you think she's instigated this? You are her best friend. She's Dee, for goodness sake. She was humiliated beyond words when he had their marriage annulled. Why would she tell him to come up to her room in the dark? You need to wake up, Jack Brewer. The man might be there to murder her. After all, if she was dead, the will would be null and void, the golden goose going to the next of kin, which would be Ray and his family.

Jack turned heel and tiptoed into the dark house, carefully skipping the stair that made the squeaking noise. He leaned against Dee's bedroom door and listened carefully.

Dee dreamed of fishing at Buckhorn with Jack. They'd caught enough for a big fish fry the next night and talked until the wee hours of the morning. Then Jack had lain back to watch the clouds skitter across the full moon. He reached out and pulled her closer to him, kissing her passionately on the lips.

"Jack." She knew even in the dream that it was just a dream. She'd wake up in a few minutes and laugh about the silliness of the whole thing.

"Darlin', you are so beautiful with the light of the moon coming through the window."

Window? They were outside on their lucky quilt, the one that Nanna had made for Jack when he was just a little boy. The moon was lovely, but there was no window. And Jack's voice was higher and didn't have its normal Okie twang. Somehow it sounded more like Ray.

"I know you still love me. You can't have fallen out of love with me so quickly. Let's have one night for old time's sake. I'll be gone before daylight. No one ever needs to know about it."

Dee's eyes popped open to find Ray sliding in the bed beside her. In her half-sleep, she sat straight up and stared at him, aghast. "What are you doing?"

He slid a hand from her knee to her thigh. "Only what you want, darling."

She scampered out of the bed on the other side. "You get out of here. Right now. What can you be thinking about, Ray? We are not married. You have a wife and a child on the way."

"I'm here, and you know you still love me. Angie doesn't have to know. We were good together, Dee."

"You are rotten to the core. I'm not stupid, Ray. You're

still trying to get me to sign those papers. You think I'm just a little ignorant country girl who's panting to get you to kiss me? Well, you are wrong. Get out of here and don't ever show your face in Murray County again. Roxie's got a shotgun, and she'd be glad to use it on you."

"Roxie doesn't scare me."

She crossed her arms over her chest and pinching herself slightly on the rib to make sure she really was awake. "How'd you get in here, anyway?"

"Remember when I came here with my fishing buddy? The key was still in the same place. We went fishing and stayed out all night, stumbled into our rooms, and got up at daybreak noon and went fishing again. I hate fishing. But I did like you, so I came back every weekend. Now come back to bed. Afterward, we'll sign those papers and I'll go away."

Outside the door, Jack listened to every word, sorry that he'd mistrusted Dee. It looked like she was holding her own without any support from anyone. However—

Jack slipped out of his flip-flops, pulled his shirt up and over his head, and threw them both on the table beside the door behind a big bouquet of asters and straw flowers. He unfastened the snap on his jean shorts and undid the zipper about an inch, slipped his boxers down inside until it appeared the shorts was all he wore. Using his fingertips, he ruffled his already unruly hair and rubbed his eyes. Then he swung the door open.

"Dee, darlin', where's Roxie keep the extra rolls of toilet paper?"

"Jack?" She was bumfuzzled. He looked like something from a beachcomber's magazine. By the light of the moon streaming in the widow, she could see his bulging biceps.

"What in the devil is going on here? I leave our bed for one minute and come back to find you with another man? Dee, is this that ex-husband of yours? What's he doing in my bed?"

Dee decided on the spur of the moment to play along. She ran to Jack's side and buried her face in a broad expanse of chest. "Jack, I'm so sorry. I didn't know he was coming back. Honest."

"Oh, yes she did. She called me and told me to come up here and we'd work out an agreement over the papers." Ray was rapidly getting out of bed and reaching for his jacket.

Jack could swear he saw a faint red glow on the man's cheeks.

"Dee? You said you were over this jerk. You promised me before we got married that you never wanted to see him again."

"You married this two-bit storekeeper? This nothing that works at the store next door? My God, Dee, I thought I'd taught you more class than that." Ray started for the door, then realized Jack was blocking it.

"This nothing person says you owe his wife an apology." Jack pushed Ray.

He bounced on the bed once and came back like a boxer ready to fight. "I won't apologize to her."

Dee felt like an actress in a soap opera. "Just let him

go, Jack. I promise it's over. We'll talk about it. Roxie will hear if there's a fight. She might shoot you in her attempt to kill Ray for coming inside her house. I couldn't bear it if I lost you because of him."

Jack stepped aside enough to let the man sneak out the door past him. "You sure?"

"You are a fool, Dee. Whatever my father paid you to get out of my life was worth every dime."

"Let him have the last word," Dee whispered so low only Jack heard it.

"I don't think so." Jack took off down the stairs.

One thing Jack had to admit when his tender bare feet hit gravel: the man could surely run fast. By the end of the driveway, when he heard the car rumble into life, he stopped the chase and gingerly picked his way back to the porch where Dee sat on the steps, waiting for him.

"I had it under control," she said between clenched teeth.

"I know." He reached into his shorts and pulled up his boxers, fastened the snap at the waistband, and zipped all the way to the top. Then he sat down beside her, keeping a healthy distance between them. One never knew when she might turn violent, even with all that pent-up anger. The last time, a flying rock found its mark and cost him a lot of blood.

"Then why'd you pull a fool stunt like that? Roxie would have had a cardiac arrest if she'd come out in the hall and found two men in my bedroom. Sometimes I get so mad at you I could just . . ."

"Come on, admit it, you haven't had so much fun

since we were kids. Maybe not since I got this scar." He pointed to the faint line on his face.

"You shouldn't have made me mad. Besides, that was twenty years ago. I was five years old and it was in broad daylight, not in the dark. Pretending to be my husband? Jack, what on earth made you do that? And where did you come from, anyway?"

"I came over to talk to you. Couldn't go to sleep with that argument or whatever-to-hell it was on my mind. Everyone was already asleep, and I sat down on the swing. Then he came up on the porch, found the spare key, and went right in."

"You thought I'd called him, didn't you?"

"For a minute."

"You don't trust me."

"And you don't trust me either."

"Trust is an issue with me right now."

"Understandable. I just did the first thing that came to my mind. Figured if he thought we were married, he'd feel like a fool."

"What you did up there wasn't half as funny as watching you chase Ray out of the yard like a stray hound dog," she giggled finally.

"Ha-ha," he said.

"But my husband? Couldn't you think of anything better? Couldn't you just have broken in with a weapon and killed him?"

"Only thing in the hall was an umbrella. I don't think he would've believed it was a sword, even in the dark, and besides, it's hard to kill a man with an umbrella."

"Got to admit the whole thing was more than a little bit childish." She leaned over and pushed him on the shoulder.

"Of course it was. But think of his place in the silly scenario. He thinks you married a geek who works at a dying convenience store after being married to the most important man on the whole east coast. That must deflate his ego somewhat."

"I hope it flattens it out like a cow patty on a flat rock in the middle of July. That will must be worth a fortune, Jack. For him to try what he did, he's desperate. And don't you be talking about my best friend like that. I don't let anyone run down Jack Brewer, not even Jack Brewer."

"Why, thank you, ma'am. I do believe my own collapsed ego is mending with that comment. I was your husband half an hour ago; now I'm relegated to the back seat and just your best friend. I may go home and eat a whole jar of Vick's VapoRub and die in a heaping bag of bones and broken heart."

"Yuck, a whole jar of Vicks would kill Freddy Krueger."

"Want to talk about it?" he asked seriously.

"What, Vicks or Ray?" she asked.

"Ray," he answered honestly.

She swatted a mosquito. "Not out here. Let's go to your place and, yes, I would like to talk about it, Jack. Very much."

He waited until they were in his kitchen. He turned

the lights on and opened the refrigerator door. "Hungry or just thirsty?"

"Dr Pepper in the can, please." Dee postponed the conversation. Why did she think she wanted to talk about it, anyway? She would make small talk, maybe go over the whole humorous episode again, and then go home.

Jack handed her a sweating can of Dr Pepper and then jerked on a T-shirt from the back of a kitchen chair. "Talk?"

"Okay. I just realized tonight why I married that man in the first place, Jack. He represented everything I wanted. A solid family. Mother. Father. Regular type of job. A home. Friends who came for dinner. All those things you read about in the magazines."

"You had that," Jack said.

"No, I didn't. I had a mother who I called Mimosa because only General Lee and God have titles. A grandmother who came to my school parties looking like a madam."

"She'll make you eat soap, she hears you talking like that."

"I know, and I'd deserve it. I fought a little girl in grade school because she said that about Roxie. Every time we had a party, she brought her beautiful petit fours and she wore all those ruffles and heels and the ratted red hair."

"You were the one who blacked Lisa's eye and bloodied her nose? You never told me. I'm hurt."

"Wasn't so proud of it. Besides, I was terrified Roxie

would find out what that kid said about her. I loved her. Still do, but I thought if you looked up the word *dysfunctional* in Webster's you'd find a family picture of me, Roxie, Mimosa, Tally, and Bodine right there beside it. A functional family, a perfect one, was like what Ray had. Life sure teaches us some hard lessons. Roxie, bless her darlin' heart, has more love in her little fingernail than those folks do in their whole body."

"Then the marriage wasn't a total failure, Dee. You learned a valuable lesson."

"I did. And I learned tonight that Ray doesn't hold one bit of my heart anymore. There's nothing there but disgust."

Jack could have shouted, but he just nodded.

"You're a good friend." She smiled, and it reached her twinkling eyes.

"Ah, shucks, I thought I made a pretty convincing husband, darlin'."

"Very convincing. Right out of *Days of Our Lives.* Check next week in *Soap Opera Digest*, and you'll find out how great the audience loved your performance. Now I'm going on back home and trying to go back to sleep. It's nice that you're still watching after me."

He opened it for her, and as she brushed past him, he reached out, gathered her into his arms, breathing in the scent of shampoo still in her hair, baby powder on her neck, and the sweet aroma of fabric softener in her nightshirt. He hugged her close, then leaned back far enough to tilt her chin up with his fist.

She tasted cold Dr Pepper in the fiery kiss. When he

released her, she leaned in slightly for more, then jerked back. What was she doing? This was Jack, her friend from next door.

He grinned. His heart soared. Something deep in his soul knew when his lips found hers that this was right. This was what he wanted forever.

"Good night, Jack," she said huskily.

"Good night, Dee," he said hoarsely.

"Maybe we'd better pretend that never happened. Just the result of the moment." If she'd known one cool kiss could set a fire to raging in her heart, she would have been wrapped up in his arms from the time she was thirteen.

"I don't think so, darlin'," he drawled as he watched her walk away.

Chapter Eight

Roxie sipped her coffee and nibbled on the corners of toast. Tally ate while she studied for a test. Dee stared out the dining room window and tried to make sense of the kiss she and Jack had shared.

Bodine appeared in the doorway and in a dramatic flourish dropped clothing and shoes on the kitchen floor.

"What's that?" Roxie asked.

Bodine poured a glass of orange juice and wrapped a piece of toast around two pieces of crisp bacon. "Ask Dee. She's the one who had two men in her bedroom last night. Didn't she wake anyone else up with the fighting?"

Tally grinned at her sister. "That's not fair. I can't even have one and you get two?"

Mimosa pushed past Bodine and rubbed sleep from

her eyes before she poured a cup of coffee. "Who gets two of what?"

"Dee had two men in her room last night. Jack left his shirt and shoes on the table beside her door," Bodine said.

Dee blushed.

Tally raised an eyebrow. "Dee?"

Roxie yawned. "Seems Ray wanted to see if he could talk her into signing those papers. I heard it all from my bedroom. Then Jack pretended to be her new husband. Ingenious act, if I do say so myself. Saved me having to load up the shotgun for the second time in one day."

"Roxie!" Dee exclaimed.

"It's over now. Got all three troubles in one twenty-four-hour period, so now we're home free." Roxie picked up the morning paper. "Looks like the weatherman is calling for cold rain today. Is Jack going with you into town to see the lawyer?"

Bodine could hardly believe her ears. "You mean Dee's not grounded or nothing? She's had men in her room and you're not even going to make clean the bathrooms or nothing?"

Roxie drew her finely arched brows down in a frown. "Little lady, who is the ultimate boss in this house?"

"You are?" Bodine sniffed.

"Then do not question my authority. Dee took care of it, along with Jack's help. You don't know everything that went on, and it's not your business. You've got a full-time job taking care of your own doorstep. Keep it swept and don't worry about anyone else's."

"What does that mean?" Bodine asked.

"It means just what it sounds like it means," Roxie told her. "You worry about keeping Bodine Hooper right and that will keep you busy enough so you won't have time to worry about other people's sins."

"Did Dee sin?" Bodine asked seriously.

"Bodine, are you jealous of me?" Dee asked.

"Yes, I am. You're all pretty and already grown up and you don't have pimples or say the wrong things or get into trouble for using bad words, and you can stay out late as you want over at Jack's house or in the porch swing," Bodine said honestly.

"Bodine, that's not nice," Tally said.

"Don't be getting on to her. I'm in the same boat as she is. I'm jealous of her," Dee said.

"You're jealous of me?" Bodine asked.

"Yes, because you're young and because you haven't made the mistakes I have, but mostly I'm jealous of Tally. I'm so jealous of her I could just have a hissy fit right here on the kitchen tile, so clean me off a space and watch me pitch one."

Tally cocked her head to one side. "Me? I just got out of jail for hot checks. I've been the poorest example of a sister in the world, and you're jealous of me?"

"Yes, I am, and do you want to know why?" Dee winked slyly at her sister.

"I've got a feeling you're about to tell me," Tally said.

"Because Bodine belongs to you and not me. I want a child, especially a daughter. Everyone in this house has a daughter but me. Roxie has one. Mimosa has two. Tally has one, and I don't have any. I want one just like Bodine, while I'm wishing, one who's a witch one day and a princess one day. Who's the only girl pirate I know. Who has a green thumb and could make silk flowers grow. That's why I'm jealous of you, Tally," Dee said.

"Wow." Bodine smiled. "I'm pretty special then, huh?"

"The most special thing in this house, young lady, and don't you forget it." Dee hugged her closely. "But not special enough the school bus will wait for you, so you'd best swallow that bacon in a hurry and get out the door. I'll be waiting at Jack's for you this afternoon. Maybe I'll even talk Roxie into letting me make peanut butter cookies today."

"I'm not just special. I'm the queen." Bodine floated on air to the front door.

"Hey, you might be the princess, but I'm not dead yet so you can't be queen," Roxie yelled at her.

"Yes, ma'am," Bodine giggled.

"Well done, Dee," Roxie said when she heard the school bus pull up in the gravel driveway. "You didn't answer my question. Is Jack going with you to the lawyer's or do you want me to go?"

"I'm going by myself. I'm twenty-five years old and I drove all the way from Pennsylvania alone, so I suppose I can get from here to Sulphur without a chaperone," Dee said.

Roxie nodded. "That's the old Hooper spirit. Besides, Jack needs to mind the store. I've got to go to Molly's this morning. You can drop me off and pick me up when you are finished."

Dee wore a pair of freshly pressed jeans, a buttoned chambray shirt, a wide leather belt, and cowboy boots.

Roxie pulled her thick red hair back with a wide silk multicolored scarf that matched her turquoise knit pants and jacket. Dee could have sworn her grandmother had been visiting a Dolly Parton garage sale.

Roxie checked her reflection in the mirror behind the sun visor and reapplied bright pink lipstick. "So what are you going to do with the inheritance?"

Dee pulled into the Brannon Inn driveway. Molly waved from the front porch. "I honestly don't know. Tell Molly I'll run in when I come back."

"That would be good. She's not faring too well these days. She's turned what business she's got lined up over to Etta, who says this is her last hunting season. She's hanging up her dishrag and cookbooks after Christmas this year."

"The B&B queens are retiring? Who's going to fill their glass slippers?"

Roxie patted her arm and picked up a basket of fresh bread and jellies. "You might be surprised. Just don't you be forgetting me. I'd hate to make you clean the bathrooms this afternoon."

"Yes, ma'am." Dee saluted.

"I'm a queen, not an army major."

"And I'm in a pickup truck so I can't curtsy. Besides, my jeans are too tight to stoop and bow."

Closing three old boardinghouses would be the end of an era in Murray County. Sure, there were bed and breakfast establishments springing up all over the area. Some in old two-story houses. Some in spare bedrooms in people's homes. And down close to Turner Falls in Davis, cabins were the in thing. Jack said there was seldom a vacancy sign flashing in the summertime. But Molly, Roxie, and Etta had begun the business fifty years ago before there were motels in every town and folks knew there was a fortune in tourist trade.

Travelers would find a place to spend the night, but what would really happen to the queens? She wondered as she nosed into one of four parking spots in front of Mamie Rockford's office. Roxie seemed to be surviving well in her self-induced retirement. Maybe the other two would as well. And what did she mean when she said what she did about who would fill their shoes? Surely Roxie didn't think Dee had come home to reopen Roxie's B&B.

Mamie met her halfway across the room. "Well, hello, Dee Hooper. You haven't changed a bit."

Dee hugged the woman. "Neither have you."

"Oh, honey, I just reduced my rates by five hundred dollars for that comment. How's Roxie and Mimosa? Haven't seen Roxie since she came in to redo her will last month, and Mimosa hasn't been by to see me since she retired." Mamie led her into an inner office.

"Roxie and Mimosa are both fine. Roxie's still the voice of the old south. She's over at Molly Branson's visiting while I'm here. Actually, I think she just made up an excuse to ride part way with me." Dee handed Mamie the papers Ray had brought. "Mimosa says she's retired and she's going to cosmetology school down in Ardmore, but I see that antsy look in her eyes. She'll be up and gone again before long."

"That's Mimosa. She's always been a free bird that couldn't sit still very long. Tell them both I said hello." Mamie scanned three pages of legal jargon.

"This is a mess. Let's make a phone call and see what's been left to you." Mamie picked up the phone and dialed the number from the top of the paper, tucked a strand of gray hair back into a bun at the nape of her neck, and bit her upper lip while she waited.

"This is Mamie Rockford from Sulphur, Oklahoma. I'm an attorney at law, representing Delylah Loretta Hooper," she said and then covered the mouthpiece and whispered, "I'm on hold while the little Chihuahua goes for the big Doberman.

"Yes, I do have the document before me and no, Ms. Hooper is not interested in signing them. My fax number is 580-622-0001 and I'll expect a full list of her inheritance in the next five minutes and a copy of the will these people have tried to dispute. That's right. No, I will not wait while you talk to Ray Suddeth. He's not back in the state anyway. Five minutes and yes, sir, I am a hard-headed southern woman."

Mamie looked up at Dee. "Tell me about this woman while we wait."

"Ray's aunt, his father's only sister, was half owner of the business they ran in Chambersburg, Pennsylvania. She was a wealthy old girl and as salty as Roxie. I loved her, and she took to me. The only one out there who did. Had a stroke a couple of years ago but before she did, she made a new will and left me what she had. Ray says the private institution used up most of her savings and worth, but there is some jewelry. I figure his new wife, Angie, has her eye on those sparkly pretties."

"I see. How are things with you and Jack?" Mamie asked.

Dee's eyes widened. "Where did that come from?"

"I see him on a monthly basis. He's got a gleam back in his eyes that don't have anything to do with bank account figures."

"We've been best friends forever and we still are."

The fax machine began to spit out sheet after sheet. "Aha. We'll save the discussion about Jack until later. Well, well, well. So the lady used up her resources in the retirement home, did she? Honey, if she did, then I'd like to see what she was worth before she signed her name on the dotted line. And the will . . . pretty simple. Says you were the most honest person she'd ever seen. The only one she could trust since her son was killed in Vietnam, and she trusted you with everything she owned. Dee, you might need some smelling salts when you see this."

Dee took the first list and scanned it. Row after row of jewelry with the appraised value in parentheses. Diamonds. Rubies. Pearls. Where on earth in Sulphur, Oklahoma, would she ever need such finery?

Mamie handed her another paper and took the jewelry list from her before she could truly comprehend everything on it. The second document reported a half a million dollars in actual cash, a portfolio of stocks and bonds worth another two million, and forty-nine percent of the company Mr. Suddeth owned.

Dee was glad she was sitting. Her mind was in a complete boggle. No wonder Ray took such a chance. No wonder Angie let him.

Mamie leaned back in her chair and looked over the top of her reading glasses. "Sounds like you've got some major decisions to make."

"Guess I do," Dee whispered. "Call him back and ask him to send me a list of the jewelry again. I want to know which pieces were hers and which were inherited from her mother. I want to know if Ray and Angie's child is a girl."

Mamie dialed the number and told the man what she wanted. "Anything else?" She turned to Dee.

"We'll be calling back in a few minutes. Soon as I see what's going on with the jewelry. I want the cash transferred into a trust account for Bodine Delight Hooper. It's to pay for her college wherever she wants to go. Set it up so that it's not something she can take out and play with. It's for college expenses. Room. Board. Books. Tuition. Monthly stipend that's generous enough to keep her from waitressing."

The fax machine began running again. Mamie picked up the new sheet and handed it to Dee. Half of the jewelry had been handed down from Ray's grandmother to her only daughter. At the end of the page was a handwritten note saying a phone call had been made to Angie who had said the ultrasound predicted a girl.

Dee wanted a daughter so badly and now Angie had that too. Anger filled her heart. "The pieces of jewelry inherited from Ray's grandmother will be put into a vault for the baby girl. The child can have the jewelry on her fortieth birthday. Not a day before. The rest of it I want delivered to me personally by a courier who'd best handcuff the briefcase to his arm and insure it to the hilt because if there's one diamond or ruby missing, I'll sue Ray. The shares in the business are up for sale to the highest bidder. That should take care of it, shouldn't it?"

"Stock portfolio? That's worth a couple of million at least. Maybe more," Mamie said.

"Ray will probably end up being her last surviving relative. Give it to him. But make it so he can't cash any of it in until he is sixty-five years old, and if he dies before his father, his wife, or even his child, it all goes to the cancer fund. If he lives to be sixty-five, it's his to do with whatever he wants."

"That's pretty decent of you. One other thing, the life insurance policy? She was insured for half a million."

"Give it to the cancer foundation. Maybe it'll help find a cure for folks like Molly."

"You sure about all this? Girl, you could be the richest woman in Murray County."

"I'm not interested in being a rich woman. I've been there and it wasn't any fun. When the shares for that company sell, put half the money in a trust for my sister

Tally, to be given to her when she graduates from college. The other half is to go to the cancer fund. I don't want any of the money, Mamie. I'll keep the jewelry that belonged to her and remember the sweet little lady who made me welcome. The rest would remind me of a very difficult time."

"Smart woman. Sign here for me to take care of everything for you, then. I expect the jewelry will arrive within a week, and that Ray will be pulling his hair out and screaming to the top of his lungs by bedtime tonight."

Dee signed with a flourish and made her still-limp legs stand up. "I certainly hope so. Thanks so much, Mamie. I appreciate you. Do I owe you anything today?"

Mamie walked her to the door. "No, if I'm going to represent you in this and take care of the trust funds, I'll just bill you later. Why don't you take a week or two to think about things? You might change your mind later."

"No, I won't. Get it all ready and call me. I'll come sign all the legal stuff then."

"Okay, then it's a done deal. The cancer foundation is going to love you, girl."

"I just wish it would have helped Molly sooner."

"I know, honey. I know. Give my best to Roxie. And tell Mimosa to call me. We'll do lunch. You know, I always envied her. She didn't give dang what people thought, and she had you. I always wanted a daughter."

"So did I," Dee whispered as she walked out the door.

Dee parked in front of Brannon's Inn. Before she

made it to the porch, Molly was at the door, holding it open for her. "Darlin' girl, I'm so glad to see you. Come right in. We're in the kitchen having oatmeal cake and coffee. Roxie's been tellin' me stories about you and Jack. I've already had two pieces of cake. Appetite sure picks up when I'm laughing." She wrapped her arms around Dee and smothered her in a hug.

Dee felt as much at home at Brannon's as she did at Roxie's. "Now don't you go believing everything Roxie tells about me."

Molly ushered Dee into the kitchen. "Roxie, pour up another cup of coffee. Next time you come around, Dee, you bring Jack with you. Haven't seen that man in a year or more."

Roxie pointed toward a chair. "So what'd you find out?"

"That there was a lot involved." Dee made noises of appreciation when she put the first bite of cake into her mouth. She told them what she'd done with the inheritance as she finished off a huge chunk of oatmeal cake.

"You just kept the jewelry for you and gave the rest away?" Molly asked.

"That's what I did."

"Think that's the wisest move," Roxie asked.

"The jewelry will remind me of a sweet lady who loved me. The rest would remind me of Ray. I don't need that." Dee dabbed her mouth with a lace-edged white napkin.

Molly cut another piece of cake and laid it in her plate. "Money isn't everything, is it? Seemed like it was when I was young, but lately it's not worth near as much. Back when I had to keep soul and body together, when my worthless husband chased everything that had a skirt on, then dollars were almighty important. But today, I can see your point. Roxie tells me you got a settlement out of the divorce that will keep you."

"Yes I did, and it's mine for seven years of stupidity. So tell me what's going on with Stella?" She changed the subject.

"She's in California. Married Mitch Mason five years ago. He's got his head in the clouds. Thinks he's movie-star pretty and he probably is, but that isn't enough to make him one of those real actors. She's working two jobs while he runs around getting something called head shots done and talks to agents about bit parts. Of course, every week when she calls, he's almost got a part. Almost don't mean squat. He's a pretty little boy in a big man's body. Only his mind didn't grow to fit the rest of him. Stella is wearing thin with him. I can tell even if she doesn't say it in so many words."

"I'm sorry. At least I thought I was happy until the bomb exploded," Dee said.

Molly waved her hands in the air. "You girls! Used to watch you and Stella and Rosie play out there in the backyard on a quilt with your doll babies. Jodie was always busy with the stick horse or using a rope to lasso the rosebushes. Figured at least three of you would grow up to be mothers and go to school parties, make cookies or cupcakes, and go to little league games right here in Murray County."

"We ain't dead yet." Dee patted her hand.

"But I would've liked to have seen it before I die."

"Now, enough of that kind of talk. You aren't going to die. After Christmas the three of us are going on a cruise. Remember?" Roxie said.

Dee cocked her head to one side. "Oh?"

"Sure we are. We've been planning it for thirty years. After Christmas every year. When hunting season is over and business slows down. Let's really do it this year," Molly said.

"I think that's wonderful," Dee said.

"I'll talk to the travel agent next week," Roxie said seriously. "You ready to go home? I bet Jack is sitting on pins. Molly got a big kick out of the story of two men in your bedroom last night."

"Roxie," Dee moaned.

"Hey, there ain't nothing in this kingdom that the queens don't share," Molly said. "It's like old times, when you girls were in high school."

The phone was ringing loudly when Roxie and Dee opened the front door. Dee grabbed it first and said, "Hello," breathlessly.

"Dee, this is Ray, you cannot do this," he said coldly.

"Do what? Where are you?"

"I'm in a taxi on my way home. I just talked to the lawyer."

"Well, Ray, I can do it and I have. The jewels are your daughter's but only when she has enough sense to appreciate their value. I figured forty was a good age for her to shed some of her mother's genes. I was generous and gave you the portfolio. It should be a good retirement fund. Take Angie around the world with it when you retire."

"The shares? For God's sake, the shares?"

"Oh, that. Well, you better find a bank with a lot of money, because they're up for sale. If I don't like the bid then I guess you can look across that big old boardroom table every Monday morning at my face and darlin', I will learn all I can about the company. You won't be pulling any wool over my eyes. Can Angie trust you to be good every week? I mean, after all, you couldn't stay away from me in Oklahoma. Buy them at the going rate or I'll fly in once a week and honey, I'll be wearing my jeans and OU T-shirts to the meetings. I didn't see a thing in the will that said anything about a black power suit."

"You wouldn't dare embarrass me and my father that way." Exasperation came through the phone.

"Yes, I definitely would. Oh, and don't call here again. I'm paying a lawyer to take care of my business. I'm sure you have her number."

"You are a worthless . . ."

"Careful there before you call me anything ugly. I could sell all those shares for a dollar to Jack Brewer and you could sit across the table from him every Monday morning."

"You wouldn't dare," he shouted.

"Ray, I really really would. Your lawyer has my lawyer's number. Tell Angie congratulations on having a daughter. I hope you both enjoy her. I always wanted a daughter. Good-bye."

"You all right?" Roxie asked from across the room.

"Never felt better. I'm going to change clothes and go see Jack."

Chapter Nine

T he store had changed little since Dee's first memories. A bit of white paint seven years ago just before she left. The old cane-bottom kitchen chair with chipped green paint had long since been relegated to the storage building out behind the trailer and replaced with a wooden bench. Everything else was the same, and that's where Dee found Jack that morning: sitting on the bench with a faraway look in his eyes.

"Hey, what happened? Was old Ray yanking your chain?"

"Yes, he was." Dee drew her knees up and rested her chin on them. Fall was in the air. Summer hadn't officially pushed it completely into the history pages, but the mornings were cooler and the thermometer was only reaching the low nineties during the day.

"So?"

"So." She sucked in a lungful of air and told the story again. "And I own forty-nine percent of the company. He called as soon as I got home. I told him he can buy them or I'll sell the whole kit and caboodle to you for a dollar bill."

"You did what?" Jack's eyes twinkled.

"Don't rush out to the bank to borrow that dollar just yet. He'll buy them."

"What's happening to that money?"

"I can't remember what I told Mamie to do with it. There's a trust fund for Bodine's education, though. And all I'm taking is the jewelry that was not part of the heritage."

"Good grief, Dee, is that what you really want? You think you ought to think about it for a while?"

"No, I was rich once. It didn't bring me a bit of happiness. You should understand that, Jack. You inherited a fortune from your grandparents and you live in a trailer, run a convenience-store-slash-bait-shop, and are happy as a lark."

Combing his hair back with his fingers, Jack nodded. "Yes, I did and yes, I am. It's nice to have enough to do what I want, but if it all went away tomorrow, the store would still support me."

"That's because you keep your lifestyle within your means."

"Trailer trash means?"

"Happiness means."

"What do you really want out of life, Dee?"

"I want . . ." She stopped and thought hard. What did

she want? She'd settled into a routine that was peaceful these past months. In what she'd always considered a dysfunctional family, that shouldn't be happening. She loved being able to run next door and talk to Jack about any and everything, and that for sure shouldn't be possible. By this time in his life he should be tied down to someone who surely wouldn't want Dee popping in at all times of the day and night.

Music drifted through the screen door leading into the store. Rascal Flatts singing a song popular a couple of years before about broken roads. She could surely relate to most of the song, something about God blessing the broken road that had led him home. It had taken a while, but she could honestly agree with the singer. It had been a long, broken road but it had eventually led her back home to Roxie, Mimosa, Tally, Bodine . . . and Jack.

"Do you know what you want?" he asked when she didn't answer.

"Yes, but I can't put it in words."

"Well, think on it for a few days. Change of subject. I have to attend a formal affair in Dallas tomorrow night. It's a yearly banquet that I'm required to dress up for. Want to go with me?"

"Sure. Cutoff jean shorts or overalls?" she teased.

"Black tie. That means something stunning, other than jean shorts and overalls, for you. Got something or do we need to leave early so you can shop?"

"I have something. What time?"

"I'll close up the store at noon. We'll get there some-time between two and two thirty. Dinner is at seven that evening with the dancing to begin at nine."

"We'll be late coming home then," she said.

"No, we'll stay the night. I've booked rooms."

"Rooms? As in more than one? You didn't need to go to that expense, Jack. We've spent nights together on the lake since we were kids. I don't reckon we'd have a problem in a hotel room with two beds."

"Speak for yourself."

Dee jerked her head around to find his eyes boring into hers. Intense sparks flew between them, leaving no room for doubt. She inhaled deeply and let it out slowly.

"Jack, I . . . ," she stammered, but the words stuck.

"I know how you feel, Dee. I'm your best friend."

"Yes, you are. I'd trust you with my life."

"But not with your heart. I had a crush on you in the fifth grade, fell in love with you our sophomore year. It wasn't just because I thought Ray was a bad choice that I tried to talk you out of eloping with him."

"That was years ago. Things change. We changed."

"But my heart didn't."

The words of the Rascal Flatts song played through her mind as if the group were standing behind her. Something about the broken roads that led her home to Jack. Those weren't the words in the song, but some-how they became the ones in her mind, keeping in per-fect time with the background music in her head.

She laid her head on her propped-up knees and shut her eyes tightly, but it didn't erase the flame of desire Jack had stirred in her with one look. "Jack, I can't go there right now."

"Just wanted you to know. Timing might not be just right, but when you get around to trusting your heart with someone, remember I'm next door. Change of subject again. Can I see the dress you are going to wear?"

"No, sir. I reserve the right to shock you."

The tension was gone. They were back on familiar footing, but for one brief second Dee wished for more. She'd suspected Jack had a crush on her at one time during their growing-up years, but for him to admit he'd loved her, that he would have trouble sleeping in the same room with her? Flattering, yes. Scary, a big yes.

"Promise you won't wear blue jeans and paint freckles on your nose." He pushed her arm, almost tumbling her out onto the wooden porch floor.

Just the touch of his palm against her bare skin sent tingles down to her toes. Guarding her heart wasn't going to be an easy feat. She'd have to stay on duty twenty-four hours a day, seven days a week.

"I promise," she said, finally.

Bodine draped her legs over the arm of the rocking chair and pouted. "I can't believe you are going away for the weekend to a glamorous place like Dallas and I have to stay home. You even get to dress up . . . ohhh, are you going to wear that?" Her eyes popped wide open at the sight of the black slinky halter dress cut high up the side and low in the front.

"I think I might. Do you like it? Pearls or diamonds?" Dee held the hanger up to her neck and swished around the room in a slow dance.

"I love it. Diamonds. Oh, yes, diamonds. You know what Miss Dolly Parton says? She says that it takes a lot of money to look that cheap. She's my newest role model. I'm going to grow up and look just like her. I'm saving my money now for blond wigs," Bodine said seriously.

"So what happened to Miss Scarlett O'Hara?" Dee slipped the dress into a garment bag, adding two others, much more discreet, just in case she changed her mind or lost her nerve. She'd bought the black dress the week before Ray came home with his annulment news and never had the chance to wear it, but it was more than a little bit risqué and had they stayed together, she would have probably never taken it out of the closet.

"I can learn a lot from Miss Scarlett, but she's not real. Miss Dolly is a real person, so I decided to be like her."

"I see." Dee grinned.

"Now, diamonds? What have you got?"

"I've got a plain little diamond drop. I wish all that stuff from Aunt Marjorie was already here . . ."

"We'll go see Roxie. A little old drop won't do. Even if it's fake diamonds, you've got to have enough to glitter and glow. Oh, and pull your hair back away from your face and put some of that glitter stuff on your shoulders." Bodine was already out the door and headed toward Roxie's bedroom.

"That's where I draw the line, young lady. I want to look classy, not trashy."

Bodine stopped in the hallway and shook her head. She'd never understand the grown-up mind, not even when she had one.

"What's going on out here?" Roxie stepped to her door.

"Dee needs diamonds 'cause she's going to the party with Jack and that aunt's jewels hasn't got here yet and she won't wear glitter on her shoulders and the dress is lovely but it's plain and . . ."

Roxie looked over Bodine's shoulder at Dee. "Okay, okay, slow down. Diamonds, huh? Go put on that dress and come back. If there's one thing I have it's a sense of style."

It was Dee's turn to roll her eyes. If she listened to Roxie and Bodine, Jack would be sending her back to the hotel room to put on her fake freckles and overalls. She took the dress from the garment bag and looped it over her arm. Roxie took it from her and hung it on the hook behind the door of her bedroom and studied it for a while.

"Uh-huh. Lovely. Provocative. Knock Jack's eyes out of his head. What are you doing, Delylah Loretta? This dress says something other than friendship to me, and I'd dare say it'll say a lot more than that to Jack."

"I'm confused right now, Roxie."

"That's all right, but remember, honey, you only got one hind end."

"What's that got to do with anything?"

"It means you got two horses you are trying to ride, Dee, and it's an impossible job since you only got one hind end to sit on the horse with. So choose your horse, Delylah. Friendship or more. I won't even ask which horse, but don't hurt that man. Now let's talk jewelry. I think a diamond choker is what you need and that's all. No glitter. No fancy stuff in your hair. Just this dress and a sparkling diamond choker." She went to a drawer, fumbled with something toward the back of it, and brought out a velvet pouch.

"What is that?" Dee asked.

"Where'd you get that and how come I've never seen it?" Bodine asked.

"One of my many secrets. It's what Dee needs for the party. A diamond choker." She brought forth a glittering choker with three rows of perfectly cut round diamonds set in white gold. "It belonged to my great-grandmother and has been passed down from one daughter to the next. I wore it on my wedding day. It's what that dress needs."

"Roxie, I can't wear that. What if the clasp broke or someone stole it? I'd be a nervous wreck."

"More nervous than deciding which horse you're going to ride?" Roxie asked.

"No. That isn't a decision. I can't ride the one I want to because it could wreck a friendship that means more to me than anything." Dee let Roxie fasten the necklace around her long, slender neck. *Stunning* was the only word that came to mind when she looked in the mirror.

"Listen to your heart," Roxie said.

"What's all this talk about horses? Can I wear that thing when I get married?" Bodine asked.

"Of course you can wear it, and the talk about horses has nothing to do with you. When you are Dee's age, you'll understand," Roxie said.

Dee reached up to touch the stones. "You should keep it in the safe deposit box, not lying in a drawer."

"There's a fake back in that drawer. Had it built in there years ago. I'm the only one who knows the combination but I put it in my will so the executor can get the jewels out. And yes, ma'am, you will wear it with that dress. No one will believe it's real anyway, so don't worry about it."

Bodine touched the velvet pouch. "What else is in there?"

Roxie shoved it back into the drawer. "Nothing that you need to see right now. It's fun to see the look in your eyes when I pull out one of my secrets, so I'm not telling everything I know today. Take the choker and wear it. Enjoy the party. When you get home, we'll talk about those horses. It's ten minutes until time to go."

"I'm more than a little bit scared."

"If you weren't I'd worry about you. There's your ride." Roxie turned Dee around to face the window.

"Great God Almighty! Is that a limo?"

"Well, it's not an Angus bull. There's more sides to Jack than a storekeeper, girl. One is he hates to drive in Dallas."

She met Jack coming up the stairs as she carried the dress and the diamonds back to her bedroom. He was dressed in perfectly creased khaki slacks, dark brown loafers, a pale yellow shirt with a light blue pinstripe, and he smelled like heaven on earth.

"I came to help carry your things. That the dress you're going to wear?"

"I'm taking three. Since it's your shindig, you can choose."

"Okay, but that one looks pretty good."

She busied herself getting the dress back into the garment bag and putting the choker in her own travel kit of jewelry. By the time she turned around, Jack had her suitcase in one hand and was holding out the other for the garment bag. She resisted the urge to check her reflection again to see how her hair looked and followed him down to the limo. The driver, a big, burly man who looked like he'd be more at home serving as bouncer in a rowdy club, stood beside the open back door. Bodine had already taken up residence, lounging back with the back of her hand on her forehead.

"This is heavenly. Please take me with you, Jack. I don't have school today since it's fall break. I'll be good and stay in the hotel room during the party. I promise."

"Okay, but if you go with me and Dee, I won't rent the limo for your Halloween festival. Which is it? A boring old grown-up party where you'll have to spend the whole weekend watching television in a hotel room, or showing off for your friends?"

Bodine crawled out in a hurry. "Sometimes I think you cheat."

"Sometimes I do." He grinned.

"I want a Hummer." She held the door open when the driver tried to shut it.

"White or black?"

"White with those sparkly lights."

"Done. Now get out of here and have a wonderful weekend, Bodine."

She blew them a kiss when the driver finally closed the door and drove away.

"You let her make you promise to spend hundreds of dollars on a Hummer limo for a night in Davis, Oklahoma?" Dee asked incredulously.

"With sparkly lights," Jack reminded her.

"Why?"

Jack sat beside Dee. "Because she likes sparkly lights, I suppose. What kind of music? Or would you prefer a movie? There's several CDs and two or three of the newest movie releases."

"I'd rather talk," she said.

"Then that's what we'll do." He opened the minibar and took out two cans of Coke.

She grabbed a can and popped the top, guzzling down a fourth of the cold drink before she came up for air with a not-so-ladylike burp.

"Done like a true redneck. I'm proud of you, honey," he drawled.

"Are you really going to get her a Hummer?"

"Sure, I am. I promised, and I'm a man of my word. Besides, I want to do it. She'll get a kick out of riding to the festival in a Hummer with her little friends."

"What are you going to do when she's a junior and going to the prom?"

"By then maybe Tally will have a good husband who'll adore Bodine and he'll take care of things. If not, I was thinking about a Cinderella carriage pulled by six white horses with gold tassels on their heads. Maybe two footmen in some kind of fancy getup to ride on the back so there'll be someone to open the door for her."

"What are you going to do if you ever have kids of your own?"

"How many do you want?" He countered right back at her.

"A houseful. One a year for the first ten years, then maybe wait about five years and then have two or three more to keep me happy in my late years. And I won't send a one of them to Mimosa or Roxie to raise."

"Sounds good to me. Want to get started this weekend on the first one?"

"Jack!" She swatted at him, almost spilling the Coke in her lap.

"Do you really want a whole bunch of kids?" he asked seriously.

"Yes, I do. What about you, Jack? You were raised as an only child. How would you cope with eight or ten children?"

"I haven't a clue but I like the idea." He leaned back and shut his eyes. The dark, cool interior of the limo usually lulled him to sleep, but every nerve in his body was on alert. He wanted to take Dee in his arms and kiss her until she begged him to start a family right that minute. He'd figured out in the past twenty-four hours what he wanted with the rest of his life, but he was a patient man . . . up to a point. "So what do you want to talk about, Dee, other than having children?"

"Why did you hire this limo?"

"Because I don't like to drive in Dallas. I hate traffic, so every year I hire someone to drive. Does that offend your sense of simple living?"

"I just figured we'd either go in the van or in my truck."

"So you don't know this old country boy quite as well as you thought." He didn't open his eyes. He didn't need to. He could see her with his eyes closed. There she was at eleven, tossing the triple hook out into the lake. Then there was the time he'd made her mad and she'd picked up a rock the size of a baseball and threw it at him. She had a pretty good aim and a dang good amount of force, hitting him in the forehead. She'd almost fainted at the sight of so much blood. By the time they'd found Roxie and Nanna, she was in hysterics. Another vision replaced that one. She wore a pink, fluffy dress at the junior prom. The next year she wore gold, and he liked it better. Then a month passed and she eloped with Ray Suddeth. If he had a dozen kids, he'd be danged sure none of them were ever named Ray.

"Penny for your thoughts." She touched his eyelids.

"Honey, you don't have enough money to buy my thoughts today."

"Jack, what is this business thing we're going to? We can talk about that, can't we?"

"Sure. It's a PR affair for all the people who work for the company I do. The good old boys who come up with new computer games. The company throws this big gala once a year. They've reserved the dining room at a five-star hotel downtown and plenty of rooms so everyone can stay that wants to do so. It'll be a late night and some of them come from Houston, fly in from New York, one from Los Angeles."

"Really?" She was amazed.

"What's the name of this company? Are you an investor?"

"I'm a heavy investor, but I don't own the thing. It's called The Corner, Incorporated. It's the business that makes and distributes the software for the computer games I design."

"It's that big?"

"Didn't start out like that, but then it grew."

"TCI? You own part of that?" She suddenly made the connection.

"Guess so," he said.

"Good lord, that's one of the up-and-coming companies right now."

"Guess so." He nodded.

"And you live . . ."

He held up a hand, "I know where I live and that I work at a convenience store. I don't like big cities. Hate 'em, matter of fact. When I was in college, I made friends with a couple of other computer geeks. We formed TCI, all legal and incorporated. It caught on like wildfire and pretty soon it was bigger than we'd ever imagined. It was big enough that we'd outgrown a small business in the backroom of Poppa's store. I opted to sell. I don't want to live in the big cities. The other two guys were Jim and Dillon. Jim wanted out completely so he took his third when we sold and bought a ranch in north Texas. Dillon and I both kept stock. So I live the way I want to around the people I choose. However, once a year I do enjoy this dinner and socializin'."

"Just once a year?" she asked.

"Well, there is the thing at Christmas. Not Christmas Eve or Christmas Day. I couldn't do that to Roxie and Bodine. It's usually the first part of the month."

"What is it?"

"A party over at Murray State College for the faculty and those who . . ." He stopped and stared out the window.

"And who?"

He took a deep breath. "I donate about ten scholarships a year to Murray State College anonymously. Nanna and Poppa left me well fixed, and I just want to help kids who don't have the means. I'm telling you my secrets, Dee."

Roxie has diamonds and who knows what else worth thousands of dollars in a hidden drawer. Jack has secrets so big they're scary. I was a rich wife once. I don't want to ride that horse again. Life sure has a way of twisting back around and biting me on the fanny.

"I think that's wonderful that you help people with their educations."

"But you don't like the man you are seeing because he's got money and you associate that with betrayal, right?"

"You know me too well."

"Then next week, I'll sell my stock in the company and give the money to the cancer foundation."

"You'd do that?"

"I told you I can live on what the store makes and what my grandparents left me. I can support ten or twelve kids on that, but if you want more than that, you'll have to do a shift at the store for me."

"Jack, you are terrible. I don't associate you with betrayal. You are my best friend, and don't you dare sell your stock. You're doing so much good with what you have. Think of all the students who'll go out in the world and be productive citizens."

"Who'll do more than sell bread and milk to the campers on their way to Buckhorn?"

"Don't ever change, Jack. I love you just the way you are." She hugged him.

He hugged back, inhaling the sweet scent of coconut shampoo and some kind of floral perfume that sent his senses reeling. When she pulled back, he tilted her face up to look into those mesmerizing aqua-colored eyes. When his lips met hers, the earth spun out of the universe and sent them flying toward heaven.

"Jack," she said hoarsely.

"You said you love me. Doesn't that warrant a kiss?" he whispered.

Warm breath filled her ear and tickled its way down the sensitive skin on the side of her neck. A knot filled her stomach and for a minute she wondered if there was some way a woman could ride two horses at one time.

"A kiss on the cheek, not one that turns my knees to jelly."

He chuckled. He might not have to be patient forever after all.

"Was that funny?" She puffed up, more out of frustration with her own feelings than anger at him.

"Little bit," he said.

"Why?"

"Dee, I like you a lot. We're friends. I missed you like the devil when you left. You were the one who didn't care if I was a nerd in high school. You were always there for me . . ."

". . . and you for me. I wasn't the most popular girl in

the Sulphur High School, if you will remember," she butted in.

"Don't fight your heart," he said simply.

"I have to, Jack. It lied to me and I don't trust it anymore."

Chapter Ten

The hotel suite had a sitting room with a bedroom off each side. Dee's room was furnished with a dark mahogany king-sized bed, matching side tables, and a bench at the end covered in the same snow-white satin as the comforter. Six fluffy pillows were stacked against the headboard. Windows and sliding doors out onto a balcony overlooking Dallas was off to her right. A doorway to the left led into a monstrous-sized bathroom with a Jacuzzi tub, separate shower, six-foot vanity with enough lights to illuminate a small town, and a walk-in closet. Her dress for the evening and two casual outfits looked lost in that much space.

She kicked off her shoes and threw herself back on the bed, laced her hands behind her head, and stared at the ceiling. Jack's question concerning what she wanted out of life haunted her thoughts, but not for long. A soft knock on the door brought her back to the moment. Jack stuck his head inside and whispered her name.

"Dee? You asleep?"

"No, I'm not," she whispered back.

He opened the door all the way. "Good. I ordered room service. I'm starving and it's a while before the banquet. Hope you still like your cheeseburgers with no onions and lots of mayonnaise."

She sat up and crossed her legs, Indian-style. "Yes, I do. Did you order tater tots?"

"Of course, and two double chocolate malts with whipped cream on top. They had strawberry swirl cheesecake, so I ordered a chunk of it too."

"My dress will never fit," she moaned.

"I don't think you'll have a problem with that. You've been able to eat as much as a football player since you were in your teens and you never have gained a pound. Here it is." He went to answer the knock on the door.

"Room service for Jack Brewer." The waiter pushed a small table into the room, unloaded its contents onto the table for two located on one end of the sitting room, collected a hefty tip from Jack, and disappeared.

Dee lifted the dome covering a white china plate and inhaled the aroma of hamburger and hot cheese, fried potatoes, and a dill pickle on the side. "Wow! That was fast. I'm starving. Sit down. Let's eat."

Jack set the second dome aside and picked up his cheeseburger. "Very different than what the chef is fixing for tonight. Not bad. Maybe not quite as good as Sonic in Sulphur, but not bad."

She nodded and kept eating. "So what's on the menu for tonight?"

"Steaks. Stuffed potatoes. Salads. The works. Then there will be a buffet of finger foods and a band and dancing after that."

"How late does the band play?"

"Until the last dog is dead or until three A.M., whichever comes first."

"You got good comfortable shoes?"

"What's that got to do with it?"

She giggled. Carefree. Happy.

He wanted to kiss her.

"I plan on dancing every one of those dances and getting all your money's worth out of the band."

"I see. Well, if my shoes start to pinch, I can always take them off and dance in my socks. What do you want to do to while away the hours until dinner time? Shop? See a museum? Name your poison. Now that you are fed and won't become a raving maniac, you get to choose."

"Me a raving maniac? If memory serves me right, Nanna always said to never let a Brewer get hungry or they might do murder. And you have the audacity to say I'm mean when I'm hungry? That would be the pot calling the kettle black."

"Did I ever tell you the story of why we came to live at the Buckhorn Corner?"

She pushed back from the table and curled up on the sofa. "No, you didn't. I figured it was because Nanna liked to fish and Poppa wanted something to do."

"That's what they let everyone think. It was really because Nanna didn't come home one night from the creek where they lived up north. Poppa didn't know how to cook or to open a can of soup so he got mean, went to the bar, and whipped every man in there. They had to run the next day or go to jail." He didn't crack so much as a hint of a smile.

"Jack! I believed you were really going to tell me a story. I trusted you." She threw a throw pillow from the sofa at him.

He ducked. It hit the silver dome and sent it skittering across the floor. So she trusted him. That was a start, anyway.

"I don't want to do one thing. I've seen museums. I don't need to shop. I want to soak up every dime this suite cost. What's on the pay-per-view? If there's nothing good, I'll read a romance book I brought along with me."

"Okay. You can read the steamy scenes out loud to me."

"You are incorrigible. For your information, this is a sweet romance. That means no steam, just a little mist. It's by an author I discovered last week. The librarian said she reads her books and they are wonderful. The title of this one is *Love Handles* and the author is Holly Jacobs."

"Love handles what?"

"Love handles everything."

"Oh, yeah. Even trust?"

"I'm not going to fight with you. That would be wasting too much money. We can fight in the middle of a green pasture, but not in a place like this. So that conversation is over. Hmmm." She polished off the last tater tot and picked up the television pamphlet from the end table. "Aha, pay-per-view has a good movie that's going to start in about five minutes. Let's watch it."

"Chick flick?"

"No. I mean yes, but no. I don't want the chick flick after all. There's a *Golden Girls* marathon on channel six. It started this morning and will go on for twelve hours."

"That's as bad as a chick flick." He picked up the remote and pushed the buttons to bring up the *Golden Girls.*

She propped her head on the overstuffed arm of the sofa and put her feet in his lap. "Are you looking for an argument? If you are, you go find a bellboy or a cleaning lady and take her outside in the middle of the parking lot and get after it. Because you're not getting one from me as long as we're in Dallas. Oh, look, Ma has a boyfriend. Isn't he cute? He looks like your Poppa."

"No, he does not," Jack argued.

"Then he doesn't." She giggled when the elderly gentleman kissed Ma on the cheek before he left.

"Roxie reminds me of Blanche," he said.

"Yep, in some ways, but she's more like Shirley MacLaine. I didn't realize it, but last week I watched that movie called *Carolina* and the grandmother in it was Roxie all over again. Then when we watched *Ru-*

mor Has It, I remember thinking that Roxie should have gone into the movies instead of the bed and break-fast business. But yes, she's like Blanche for attitude. She and Blanche could be sisters but don't tell Blanche that. She'd think Roxie should be her mother."

He sighed. He really wasn't going to get a rise out of her. She laughed at the one-liners from Blanche, Dorothy, Rose, and Ma, and he promptly fell asleep.

Jack was completely dressed in his black tux, except for the jacket that he'd slung over his shoulder, when he opened the door from his bedroom into the sitting room. Dee turned when she heard the noise of a closing door, and his mouth went dry. Framed in the open balcony doors with the sun behind her, providing shimmering highlights in her hair and silhouetting a near-perfect figure, she cocked her head off to one side. He'd never seen her look so feminine, so desirable, in his life.

She crossed the room and touched his arm. "Well, don't you just look like man in *GQ*."

"Thank you. And you are very beautiful. I forgot my Taser gun to keep the men at arm's length away from you."

"Oh, they'll just be eyeballing Roxie's necklace and trying to figure out a way to steal it."

He slipped on the jacket and offered her his arm. "Keep thinking that, Dee. Just keep right on thinking that. Shall we go knock them all dead?"

She looped her arm into his and avoided looking up

into his face. "Sure. Then we'll hide out at Buckhorn Corner and they'll never find us."

Keep it light. Friendly and light. Chase down your racing heart and put some chains on it. This would never work, and you know it. So tease Jack and keep his friendship, but don't let it go any further than that.

The dining room went silent as a tomb when they appeared in the doorway. Women's eyes looked disappointed; men's raked up and down, from Dee's hair to her toes, scarcely stopping to admire the sparkling diamonds around her neck.

"Are they breathing still or did they all die?" she mumbled out the corner of her mouth.

"They're stunned speechless at your beauty."

"Flattery will get you everywhere."

"Well, why didn't you tell me that before now?"

"Hello, Jack." A man was suddenly at his side, leaving no doubt from his wandering eyes that his interest was in Dee, not Jack.

"Hello, Dillon. This is Delylah Hooper. Delylah, this is Dillon Watterson, one of the other stockholders and game inventors in the company."

Dillon took her hand in his and raised the fingertips to his lips. "It's a pleasure to meet you. And no sign of a wedding ring? Does that mean . . ."

"It means she's with me this evening." Jack slipped his arm around Dee's shoulders and led her into the room.

A low buzz began to hover around the shoulders of the men and women, everyone wondering who Jack had brought to the reception. For five years they'd all been coming to this party, and he'd arrived alone every time.

"So did you find out who she is?" one of the men whispered to Dillon.

"She's a gold digger. See that fake necklace and the look in her eye? Her name is Delylah Hooper. Is that a real name or what? She's a beauty, isn't she, but she's as fake as a two-dollar bill. We'll have to save Jack from himself, I'm afraid. He's so innocent he doesn't even know when a woman is out to fleece him." Dillon stared at her.

"What is that man's problem?" Dee asked Jack. "He's the rudest person I've ever met and honey, I've been around some really sly critters."

"Oh, don't mind Dillon. He's just jealous. Oh, hello, Marshall. How are you this evening? I'd like you to meet Delylah Hooper. This is Marshall Smith, one of the engineers for the company." Jack shook hands with a middle-aged, white-haired man who'd appeared beside him.

"A pleasure, Miss Hooper. Come and meet my wife. I'm sure you'd rather talk girl talk than listen to us, and I'd like a moment with Jack. Candace, honey, this is Delylah Hooper. She's with Jack. Introduce her to the wives while we talk shop for a while." Marshall touched his wife's arm.

A tall woman with brown hair styled in a chin-length pageboy and hazel eyes steered her toward a group introduced her to several women standing in a circle.

"This is Marylee, Cindy, Darla, and Eva. We are the engineers' wives. That circle over there would be the board of directors' wives, and those ladies over there are investors' wives."

"So nice to meet you all. Marylee. Cindy. Darla and Eva." She said all their names aloud and hoped she would remember them. "Which wife belongs to Dillon?"

"Dillon is not married. He and Jack are not husband material. Who'd want to be married to a computer geek who'd rather design games than take his wife out to dinner?" Marylee said.

"Maybe someone who loved the computer geek?" Dee said shortly before she thought and then wished she could take the words back.

"So are things serious between you and Jack?" Marylee asked.

"We are very good friends," Dee said.

"I bet you are," Eva said. "Lots of women would probably like to be his very good friend."

The conversation strayed in a hurry to what the women were going to do with the rest of the weekend. Dee caught Jack's eye one time, and he winked.

Half an hour later, people began to find their seats around tables for four. Marshall and Candace were seated with Dee and Jack. Talk went to the weather, how unbearably hot the summer had been, the swimming pool Marshall was putting in for their grandchildren, and the new housing development they were looking at near McKinney. Candace excused herself, went to the ladies' room, and returned within a few minutes.

"So, what do you do for a living?" Candace looked right at Dee.

"Oh, I don't do anything right now. I help Jack sometimes at the store and keep Roxie, that's my grandmother, company," Dee answered.

Sarcasm dripped from Candace's lips like honey from a beehive. "Really? No children. No job. Must be nice. I would have figured you for a model or maybe a high-powered lawyer."

"What do you do?" Dee had tamed professional shrews. Candace barely fit into the amateur category.

"I got my doctorate degree in journalism, worked as a newspaper editor for twenty years while I raised my two sons, and now I teach here in Dallas. I've never had the luxury of doing nothing, but then I'd go stark raving mad with boredom if I didn't contribute to society. Do you ever plan to do an honest day's work?"

"Oh, I think I do an honest day's work pretty often. No one complains too loudly, do they, Jack?" Dee wasn't going to let Candace intimidate her but wondered why the woman had suddenly turned so cold. Dee hadn't eaten with the wrong fork or picked her nose during dinner. She'd been careful not to sop up the gravy with a biscuit or eat her salad with her fingers.

Jack felt the tension but couldn't imagine what had turned Candace into a first-rate witch. Of all the women in the group, she had always been the mother hen.

Surely she wasn't upset because he'd brought Dee without saying anything to her. "Dee works hard at what she does," he said tersely.

"I'm sure she does," Candace said.

"What bug bit you in the women's room?" Jack asked her bluntly.

She shook her finger under his nose. "You know exactly what I'm talking about, young man."

"Candace, what in the hell are you talking about?" Jack drew his eyes down in a serious frown.

"I'd like some kind of explanation too." Marshall's face was scarlet, his white hair looking even paler against the blush.

"I'm not talking to either of you," Candace declared and stormed off to the ladies' room. Immediately, Darla, Eva, Cindy, and Marylee left their tables and joined her for the second time that evening.

"Think you should go straighten that out?" Jack asked Dee.

"No, sir. I wouldn't go in there without a pistol. You haven't got enough money in your bank account to send me in there with that den of vipers. No offense, Marshall. I have no idea what I did wrong. What did I do wrong? Do I have food in my teeth?"

"My apologies," Marshall muttered.

The tension was eased slightly when the band began to play and several women dragged their husbands or boyfriends out onto the dance floor. Dee stood up and held her hand out to Jack. "I do believe you promised to dance with me until we both ended up in our sock feet before we went to bed."

"I guess I did. Excuse me, Marshall. I'm sure this is a misunderstanding, and it will be settled in there." Jack nodded toward the bathroom.

"I hope so. I haven't seen her act like that since the time she got it in her head I was having an affair with my secretary," Marshall said.

"Do you think she thought I was flirting with you?" Dee asked.

"Surely not," Marshall laughed. "I wouldn't be that lucky."

Jack shook his head in bewilderment and led Dee out onto the floor. They danced half a dozen times before settling into comfortable bar stools to catch their breath.

"I'm still getting glances like I'm a leper," Dee whispered.

"Don't worry. Maybe Candace had another woman lined up for me tonight. It's always been a big joke about how I never have a date."

Dillon showed up at her side. "Well, hellll-o. I was wondering if I might steal this beauty from you for a while, Jack. One dance and then I'll bring her right back."

"Of course." Dee set down the stemmed glass and let Dillon take her out onto the floor for a slow song.

Jack's heart constricted into a knot of jealousy. Dillon was the old proverbial tall, dark, and handsome. He worked out continually, was well traveled and educated, a smooth talker. He'd have Dee hanging on every word before the song ended and flying off to Paris to eat French cuisine within a week. Then he'd dump her, and Jack would have to pick up the pieces. Was that to be his fate? Always the friend; never the boyfriend.

Dillon asked as they moved effortlessly together around the dance floor. "So who taught you to dance? You must have had lessons as well as you do this."

"No, just a love for dancing." Dee wiggled a bit to put a little more room between them.

"How much?" Dillon asked.

"For what?" she asked right back.

"To make you go away and forget all about Jack. He's my good friend, and I don't want to see him hurt. You're just a little gold digger. You've found out he has money, and you're out to take him. It's plain as day." He tried to draw her back tighter into his arms.

"Would you explain what you are talking about?" She looked around for Jack, who was no where to be seen.

"I'm asking you what I would have to pay you to walk away from him?"

"Why?"

"Because he is my friend and I don't want to see him taken in by the likes of you. I know women. I've been around the clubhouse corner lots of times. Jack trusts too easily when it comes to women. I've been protecting him for years. It's cost me a few dollars but, hey, I figure they were well spent," Dillon said gruffly.

"I. Am. Not. A. Gold. Digger." Steam all but flew from her ears and eyes.

"Oh, sure, you aren't."

She inhaled deeply, clenched her hands into fists, and pushed herself out of Dillon's arms. The whole thing with Candace suddenly made sense. All of Jack's important friends thought she was just interested in his money. She couldn't stay there in that kind of tension. Holding her head high and her back stiff, she resolutely walked off the dance floor, through the lobby, and to the elevators. By the time she got to her room, big black tears were streaming down her face. She stopped at the sofa, picked up the phone, and called the front desk.

"Would you please have a taxi waiting for me in five minutes?"

Then she went to her room, jerked off her fancy dress, and threw it into the suitcase along with the diamond necklace. She was wearing jeans and a T-shirt when she rode the elevator down to the first floor and walked out to find her taxi waiting. She crawled into the back and suddenly didn't know where to have him drive her.

"Where to, ma'am?" He turned to face her.

"Take me to the bus station."

"Yes, ma'am."

She missed the first bus north by ten minutes and had to wait half an hour for the next one going to Oklahoma City. The station manager said the bus went straight up Interstate 35 and would stop at a service station just off exit 55, only fourteen miles from Sulphur, but she'd have to pay the full fare to Oklahoma City. Carrying her suitcase with her, she went to the bathroom, washed her face, removing all the makeup, and put Roxie's necklace in the zippered compartment of her purse. She'd have to check the suitcase and with the way her luck was running, she'd end up losing the thing.

The bus was only about half full, so she had a seat to herself. What had started out as a perfect evening had suddenly turned into a nightmare. For two hours she stared out the window at the darkness and wondered what Dillon had seen in her to make him think such a thing. She didn't have a single answer when they reached the exit.

She used the pay phone and called Roxie who said she'd be there in half an hour to pick her up, then she sat down in a booth and drank a cup of strong coffee. Business was slow. Two people came in for an A&W Root Beer float. A couple of cars were filled up with gas. But other than that, she was alone in the station-store combination. Roxie arrived just as she finished the last drop of coffee. She picked up the suitcase and pulled it along behind her out to the white Cadillac.

"So what is this all about?" Roxie asked. "Did Jack die?"

"No, but he might when he gets home. His friends all think I'm a gold digger. His friend Candace was so rude it was awful, and he disappeared when they hauled me to the lion's den."

"What did you do?"

"I didn't understand what Candace was talking about. And I sure didn't understand what Dillon was saying until he spelled it out for me. That's why everyone was staring at me and frowning. Why would Jack let them think I was that kind of person?"

"I don't believe he did. Did you confront him?"

"No, I just ran away. He's my best friend, and I couldn't face him or any of them. It was horrible. I've never been treated so rudely in my whole life. It reminded me of the feelings I had when Ray came in and told me we were annulled and he was marrying Angie. The pit of my stomach felt like I'd swallowed acid. I just called a taxi and caught a bus home."

"We'll get it all straightened out tomorrow."

Dee buried her face in her hands and broke into a fresh batch of wracking sobs.

Jack checked his reflection in the bathroom mirror and ran his fingers through his hair. He'd been nice and let Dillon dance with Dee once, just because he needed to make a run to the men's room, but he'd be hanged if he let anyone else claim her for even one dance.

He walked out and scanned the dance floor and bar for her. Evidently, she'd had to go to the ladies' room right after the dance finished. He just hoped the old cats were finished clawing their way through whatever burr was in their saddle before she went inside. Hurriedly, he located all five of them, sitting together at the bar, their heads together.

"Good," he said aloud. At least they wouldn't have Dee cornered. However, if they did, he'd put his money on the girl. She could probably single-handedly take them all on and come out the winner.

He grabbed a bar stool as far away from them as possible and ordered a Coke.

"Hello. Hope you didn't like that girl." Dillon claimed a seat beside him.

"What?" Jack turned to face him.

"I upset her, and she took off like a scalded hound. Marylee said she saw her getting in a taxi just a few minutes ago and hightailing it out of here," Dillon said.

"Dee is gone?"

"Yes, I'm sorry. It's my fault but I just voiced what we all already figured out. I did you a big favor, again."

"What are you saying?" Jack asked.

"Can't anyone understand me? She acted dumb and now you are too. Candace could see through her. Eva knew the minute she spoke to the girl. Marylee said that she didn't fool her for a minute. Can't you see that she was just after your money?"

Jack's fist shot out and clipped Dillon on the jaw, knocking him to the floor. "You fool. Whatever made you say that about her? She's been my best friend forever."

"She's not your friend, Jack. She's after your money. I could see it. We all could. I was just protecting your interests." Dillon rubbed his jaw and righted himself back onto the bar stool.

Everyone in the place stopped and stared at Jack.

"For your information, Dee Hooper lives next door to me in Oklahoma on Buckhorn Corner. I've known her my whole life. We grew up together, and she's not after my money."

"Jack, I'm so sorry," Dillon said. "I just figured . . ."

"You just figured wrong and don't apologize to me. It's Dee who you've hurt."

"Jack, it was an honest mistake. We were just trying to be your friends and protect you," Marshall said.

"I don't need your protection or your friendship if this is the way it goes. That was a malicious mistake. You could have asked me, Dillon. I'm leaving and hopefully I'll find her. And don't go meddling in my business ever again. Is that understood?"

Dillon nodded.

Chapter Eleven

Dee gathered the quilt tightly around her and snuggled down into the porch swing. She'd gone to bed but tossed and tumbled, unable to sleep, so she'd gone outside, dragging the quilt from her bed behind her. Thoughts kept running an endless circle around her mind. What she should have done, which was stay and confront the whole lot of them. What she surely should not have done, which was run away and let them all think they were right. What she'd say to Jack. Why hadn't she thrown a fit right there on the dance floor? Like a screaming fishwife, slapping Dillon and maybe even Candace.

The crunch of gravel under the tires of the limo brought her out of the "what-if" world and back into reality. The white automobile sparkled in the light of the moon and even though Dee was angry at Jack, she couldn't keep from watching. He tossed his suitcase at the porch, peeled several bills from a money clip and handed it to the driver, and then promptly marched toward Roxie's.

Just as he raised his hand to knock on the door at three o'clock in the morning, she spoke. "Are you looking for me?"

"Yes, I am." He sat down on the swing.

She pulled her feet back so he wouldn't touch her.

He sighed. "It was all a big, big mistake. . . ."

"I should have decked Dillon. Take me back down there and I'll march right into his room, drag him out of bed, and beat him until he's cold."

"I did deck him. I am so sorry for all this, Dee. I'm never leaving the Corner again. It's not worth it. I may sell every dime of my stock in TCI."

"I didn't trust you after all. I shouldn't have run away." The truth settled like a heavy shroud around her, smothering the breath from her lungs, causing her heart to ache.

He cocked his head off to one side and stared at her. "What did you say?"

"Trust. It all boils down to trust, doesn't it? I should have plowed right into that bathroom and straightened it out with those women, but I didn't want to cause a scene. Ray would have died on the spot if I'd ever put a ripple in the water, so I learned to ignore women like Candace. Then when Dillon accused me of being after your money and said he was always protecting you from women, I ran away without even confronting you and not slapping fire into his cheeks either. I said the other day I trusted you, but evidently I didn't."

"Me neither, Dee. When you were out there with Dillon on the dance floor, a part of me was terrified that you'd let him talk you into a date and then you'd run away with him like you did Ray. I didn't trust you either. I figured he was so smooth and slick that he could talk you into anything. What did you just say? That he's always protecting me from women? Well, that sure as hell explains a lot."

"That scoundrel? He's slick but slick as in slimy, not as in desirable."

"So what do we do? I was miserable the whole way home, worrying that you'd been mugged or hurt. Someone saw you leave so I got in touch with the cab company, who traced your destination to the bus station. I missed your bus by an hour, so I just called the limo service and came home."

She stretched her feet out and put them in his lap. "What do we do? We go on. It was a terrible weekend. Roxie says that which does not kill us makes us stronger."

He tucked the quilt more firmly around her toes. "I don't feel stronger. I'm still angry at Dillon and all the rest of them."

"Don't sell your stock because you are angry. You are doing too much good with your money. Think of all those kids who are getting an education."

"Okay, but I'm going to stay right here in my corner of the world."

"Me too," she sighed.

"Are we back to normal?"

"I don't know. What's normal?"

"I'm not sure, but I know I was jealous tonight. The only other time I can remember feeling like this is the night you eloped."

"Jack . . ."

"Don't say a word. I don't want a long-winded 'I'm your friend' speech. I'm tired. I'm glad you're home. I'm sorry for what happened. I'm going home and to sleep. Want to go fishing tomorrow afternoon? I've already planned on having the day off."

She nodded.

"Is that a yes?"

"You told me not to say a word," she reminded him curtly.

"Come over and beat on the door when you wake up," he replied with the same amount of icy undertone.

"Are we parting company still mad at each other?"

"I'm not mad at you. I'm mad at me for wanting what I can't have."

He left her speechless on the swing.

She gathered her quilt around her body and went inside, made her way gingerly around furniture to the living room, and curled up in a chair in a dark corner, flipped on the lamp beside her and jumped two feet straight up. Roxie was sitting in a rocking chair not two feet away. Pink sponge curlers covered her head. She wore some kind of whitish-green mask on her face. Her yellow satin caftan had splashes of red flowers the size

of dinner plates all over it. One yellow satin slipper
with marabou trip and two-inch heels dangled from the
end of her right foot, which was slung over the leg of
the chair.

"So do we get two shovels and bury him, or did he
have some kind of tale to tell that kept his heart beating
a while longer?" Roxie asked.

"I don't know about his heart, but mine just stopped
when I saw you."

"Don't get testy, girl. Tell me what happened."

"He hit the man who hurt my feelings and came
home."

"Those people must have the IQ of a box of
rocks. . . ."

"They were so mean," Dee said.

"Upset you awful, didn't it?" Roxie sat still.

"Yes, it did."

"Why didn't you go right then and jump in the middle of him? I think you care about that man and you're
afraid to trust him. That's what I think."

"I think you are right. I do care about Jack. I love
him, but I'm not going to get romantically involved
with him, Roxie, because I do love him. You can see
what happened tonight. I couldn't bear it if we lived together seven years and he walked in one day and said he
didn't love me, that there was another woman. I'd die."

"Probably not. He would be dead, because I'd kill
him for sure. It's tough isn't it? You don't get seven
years or even seven minutes. You only get now. The
past, with its failures and triumphs, is gone. The future

is just a bright star in the sky. Today is what you've got. Learn to trust your heart, Dee."

"That's what Jack said, but it lied to me with Ray and I'll never trust it again." Dee dabbed at her red, swollen eyes.

"Your heart never lied to you, girl. You ignored it and me, both. Now, I am going to bed. Couldn't sleep, knowing you were out there fighting with Jack. You'd do well to get some rest. You look like hell warmed over on Sunday morning."

"Thank you so much." Dee followed her up the stairs.

"Truth is truth whether you like it or not." Roxie had the last word as she shut the door to her bedroom.

Dee lay awake until the sun was a big orange ball outside her window, then finally she shut her eyes and slept.

Jack and Dee sat on the curb outside the haunted house listening to Bodine scream louder than anyone else. Dee drew a bright-pink zippered sweatshirt tight around her when the north wind picked up. At least it was a cool night. When Indian summer claimed its rights at the end of October, sometimes the festivals were hot as a July day. Dee liked the cool, crisp fall weather much better.

Murray County had two Halloween festivals: one in Davis and one in Sulphur. Roxie had brought Dee and Tally to both every year when they were little. She could well remember being the girl in the haunted house with the best set of lungs, as well as being the girl in the classroom with no voice the next day. Roxie had opted to stay with Molly that year. Tally had midterm tests to study for. Mimosa had a date with some guy she met at a coffee shop in Ardmore. That left Jack, who'd already promised Bodine a Hummer limousine for the evening. She'd decided two days before Halloween that she'd be satisfied with a plain old limo rented from an agency right there in Davis, if she could bring extra friends. So Jack and Dee were entertaining five little girls and a big white Hummer limo was parked just around the corner beside the *Davis News* building.

"Cold?" Jack asked between bites of a Frito chili pie.

"A little," she admitted.

He threw an arm around her, drawing her close to his side. "Here, eat a few bites of this. It'll warm you right up." He fed her an overloaded spoon of the chili mixture.

"Good Lord, what is that?" She chewed fast and swallowed hard, grabbing for his canned Dr Pepper before she blew fire like a dragon.

"I stopped by the nacho booth and bought a side order of jalapeños for my chili pie. Warms it up, don't it?"

"Sets it on fire."

"Dee, I need my purse to get some more money. We want to go to the haunted house again." Bodine and her friends jumped around in front of her.

"Did you all eat the Energizer Bunny in that place?" Jack asked.

"Oh, Jack, you're so funny," Clarissa, Bodine's friend, said.

Bodine took money from her purse and then handed it back to Dee for safekeeping. "We just got another hour and then we have to go home. We want to do the haunted house again and then we're going to find something to eat. What's that you got? Frito chili pie? That's what I want when we come out."

Jack loaded up the spoon and shoved it toward Bodine, who opened her mouth like a little bird. "Here, have a taste."

She waved her hand in front of her mouth dramatically "Great balls of fire!"

Dee laughed. "Well said. He put peppers in it."

"You aren't funny anymore. Give me that Dr Pepper." Bodine danced around like the heat from the peppers had settled in her feet.

"So, has the last five hours cured you of wanting a house full of kids?" Jack asked.

"No, it has not," Dee said.

"So when do we start the first one?"

"Soon as the fire dies from the chili pie."

"Honestly?" Jack raised an eyebrow.

"Honestly? No."

"Why?"

"Because I do love you. I've told you a thousand times, I wouldn't jeopardize our friendship for anything. Not even for the chance of a whole houseful of kids with you."

"Has to be friendship only, then? Can't be anything more? Not even when I cold-cocked Dillon, threatened to sell my stock, and let you catch more fish than me the next day?"

"I don't want to ever live without your friendship again, Jack. I want to come tell you all my secrets and sit on the porch and watch fireflies. I don't want to lose that when the love dies. And you did not let me catch more fish. I'm a better fisherman than you are."

"But you're not really sure, are you? I could have put some kind of potion on your bait that lured the fish to your hook instead of mine, and then you sit here and tell me you love me as a brother. My heart is broken."

So it wasn't that she didn't love him or couldn't. It wasn't because she saw a boy with bony knees and thick glasses. It was simply that she hadn't figured out she could have both friendship and passion. It had been less than four months since she'd come home from Pennsylvania. She'd come a long way in that time. They'd even gotten past the disastrous evening in Dallas the previous week. He'd feared she'd never speak to him again, but they'd gotten over that hurdle and even the awkwardness of the next few days. At least they were back to the point where they'd been before the Dallas fiasco.

"Hey, you two. Fancy meeting you here." A tall, blond woman claimed a piece of the curb right beside Dee.

"Jodie Cahill. You haven't changed a bit. What are you doing at the Davis Halloween Carnival?" Dee smiled brightly.

"Just taking in all the excitement. Granny Etta and I did the Sulphur one last night. She and the ladies of her club sell barbecue sandwiches. It's their major fundraiser for the year. I heard you'd come home. Roxie said you were so bullheaded it took seven years for you to admit you were wrong." Jodie pushed a weathered cowboy hat to the back of her head.

"Can't ever be said that Roxie sugarcoats the situation, can it?"

"Not one of the queens would ever sugarcoat anything. They're famous for being big-mouthed and honest to the point of cruelty." Jodie grinned.

"So you married?"

"Me? No, ma'am. What man wants a ranchin' woman who rides bulls and sings in a honky-tonk on Friday and Saturday nights? They want a simpering little wife who can't change a light bulb."

"Not me," Jack said.

Jodie reached around Dee and patted him on the shoulder. "I wasn't talkin' about you, darlin'. I'm talkin' about men in general."

"Well, thank goodness I'm not men in general. Of course, if I thought you'd set your hat for me, my run gear would take off like a greased pig at the county fair."

"I know that, but we won't tell Dee that you're a wuss," Jodie said.

"I'm going to go find one of Etta's barbecue sandwiches and leave you girls to discuss the finer points of the sensitive male ego." Jack disappeared into the nippy fall night air.

"So what do you hear from Roseanna?" Dee asked.

"Rosy is unhappy. Looks like not a one of you girls got a marriage that'll make the golden years. Granny Brannon says Stella is hanging on by a thread. That actor she married is worthless. Rosy is so homesick she could cry, but she sticks with it, hoping that one day Trey will say they buy a ranch up around Tulsa where she can have horses and cows. It ain't happening. I go up there every few months to that penthouse in the middle of downtown. It is not a pretty sight."

"That why you aren't married? Did the three older bed and breakfast granddaughters sour you on men?" Dee asked.

Was that Marla talking to Jack? Dee squinted, looking past clusters of people, across the street. Yes, it was Marla, and she was whispering something in Jack's ear. Dee could feel herself turning a mossy shade of green. But she'd just laid down the law concerning Jack and the future. If he wanted to reconsider and marry Marla after all, if he wanted to move from Buckhorn Corner into town and be the mayor of Sulphur, if he wanted to have a yard full of kids with Marla, then Delylah Loretta Hooper couldn't say a word.

She'd lose his friendship because Marla would never understand a relationship like they had. Dee wasn't sure she understood it, but a hollow spot in her heart grew so big that she felt a great cold gulf where a warm core had been just minutes before.

Jodie touched her arm. "Hey, you haven't heard a thing I said. You all right?"

"I'm sorry." Dee blushed.

"He is handsome, isn't he? Grew up to be a fine-looking man even though I had my doubts for a while. Thought he might never grow into those lanky old bones. I wondered why you two never got together. You were always the best of friends. Even closer than you were with Stella and Rosy."

"That's the reason, Jodie. We're friends. I love him too much to ruin it." Dee was miserable watching Marla touch Jack's arm and gaze up into his eyes.

"Honey, you got a lot to learn. Just don't let something slip through your fingers while you're trying to figure out things." Jodie stood up and disappeared into the crowd gathering around the front of the spookhouse.

"Was that Marla?" Dee asked when Jack joined her on the curb.

"Yep." He ate a barbecue sandwich, wiped his chin on a paper towel, and popped the top on another soft drink. "I love these carnivals. Eat too much and then have to swallow half a bottle of Tums, but it's worth every bit of it."

"So?"

"So what?"

"She looked like she could bypass all the good food and eat Tums off your naked body."

"Jealous?"

"As hell," Dee said.

Jack chuckled. "You don't have anything to worry about. She's not getting cold feet. Besides, she wants to make her husband the mayor and then maybe a governor. I think she has her eyes set on the White House."

"She would never understand our friendship," Dee said.

"I don't think I do either," he said honestly.

Bodine and her friends arrived like a whirlwind and sorted out their purses from the pile beside Dee. "Hey, we're going to eat and then we'll be ready to go home. This has been the best festival ever. That haunted house scared the devil out of us."

"Then we can expect little angels in church tomorrow morning?" Jack asked.

"We're always angels." Bodine blinked innocently. "Can we keep the limo to take us to church tomorrow?"

"No, ma'am, you cannot," Jack said. "But right now you can all go load up in it one more time and we'll make a few loops around Davis and Sulphur before we take the ladies home for the night."

"It's been wonderful, hasn't it?" Clarissa sighed. "I feel like a princess."

"Me too," chimed in the rest of the girls.

The driver delivered all of Bodine's friends to their front doors, then took Dee, Bodine, and Jack out to Buckhorn Corner. Bodine ran into the house to tell her mother all about the evening, and Dee walked across the lawns toward the trailer with Jack.

Mimosa sat in the shadows on the bench in front of the store. "Hey, you two."

"What are you doing out here?" Dee asked.

"Waiting on you. I can't do it, Dee. I just can't do it."

"What are you talking about, Mimosa?" Jack asked.

"When are you leaving?" Dee asked.

"In about thirty minutes. His name is Fred and he owns his truck. I'll be the other team driver. We'll be getting married day after tomorrow in Las Vegas. We've got a haul through there to Los Angeles. I thought I could retire and stay home, but I can't. Roxie doesn't need me. Not yet. I feel like I'm suffocating in this place. The desire to run has been so bad this past week I thought I'd die. Fred's been pestering me for three months to go on the road with him. His partner quit last week and . . . well, I just wanted you to tell Roxie for me when she comes home from Molly's."

"You tell her," Dee said.

"I can't. Never could. That's why I always run away at night or when she's gone. I hear the truck coming up the road now. Fred isn't going to pull into the drive. Tell her I love her but I just can't retire yet. Come give your Momma a hug, darlin'. I'll call every Friday night. That's what Roxie is used to. She'll be looking for the call. Oh, and here's my cell phone number, and Fred's truck license number and everything else you might need."

"Mimosa, don't go. Stay here and fight this. Sure, you get the urge to run. We all do. But we'll be your support group." Dee begged.

"Can't do it, darlin'. I'll die if I don't get away." Mimosa picked up her suitcase and waved as she jogged down the lane to the waiting semi.

"It lasted four months this time. That's a record," Jack said.

Dee sat down on the bench and drew her knees up to her chin. "I think for the first time I understand my mother."

"You feel the need to run?" Jack leaned against the porch post.

"Not now, but I did seven years ago. Anything to get away from Buckhorn Corner, from Sulphur, even from Roxie. Then again, when Ray lowered that megabomb on me, the only place I could think to run to was right back home."

Jack moved to the bench and took her hand in his, holding it there, liking the feel of soft skin and small fingers in his big hand. "I'm glad you don't feel the need to run anymore."

She leaned her head over to rest on his shoulder. "So am I, Jack. Be that as it may, it's home and I'm glad to be here."

"Want me to tell Roxie when she comes home?"

"No. I'll do it. Roxie won't be surprised. She liked having us all home for a while, but in the back of her mind, I'm sure she knew it was coming. Mimosa has been antsy for weeks now. We could all see it."

"Think Tally and Bodine will ever move?" He sat very still. The closeness of her was enough for that night.

"In time. Tally's been talking more and more about this one professor and she's studying really hard to make good grades. I think she's grown up and found herself. She'll be a good mother to Bodine, and after all that's gone on in Murray County, she'd be wise to move away. I hope she finds happiness," Dee said.

"And you?"

"I'm the granddaughter who's going to stay around and take care of Roxie. I've been down the broken road running from life and searching for the perfect family. The crazy thing circled right back around to this corner. I guess I found what I was looking for. I'm not leaving. The need to run isn't there anymore."

Chapter Twelve

The weather was perfect for Thanksgiving. Just enough bite in the air to let everyone know fall had pushed summer into the history pages, but enough sunshine peeping through the floating clouds to make the maple tree leaves sparkle. The red house on Buckhorn Corner was filled with the aroma of pies, cakes, ham, turkey, and hot rolls. Roxie was the general, and the rest of the family followed her orders.

Votive candles in ceramic pumpkins burned brightly on the sideboard, blending their warm vanilla odor to those coming from the kitchen. The ivory damask tablecloth and matching napkins had been taken out of storage, washed, and carefully ironed. Now they graced the dining room table, along with the best china, silverware, and crystal.

"Roxie, why are we doing all this?" Bodine asked.

"Last Thanksgiving we fixed a little bitty chicken and some dressing for Jack and me and you, and we ate in the kitchen."

"This is one of our blessin' days, child. We've got a full house coming for dinner today. Now you get busy and make the relish tray. Pickled okra and zucchini, watermelon rind pickles, and some of those little grape tomatoes for color." Roxie basted the turkey one more time.

"What if I don't like him?" Bodine chose her favorite pickle dish. The divided one with three compartments. "What if he don't like me?"

"Then we'll drown him in the lake," Dee said from the stove where she stirred the baked beans simmering on a back burner. "Anyone who doesn't like you doesn't deserve to eat Roxie's good dinner."

Bodine giggled. "Can we drown Fred too, so Mimosa will come back home?"

"Sure," Dee said. "How dare men think they can waltz right into our lives, steal our families right from under our noses, and we'll still be all happy and sweet?"

"What men?" Jack caught the tail end of the conversation as he came in the back door.

"Not you," Bodine wiped her hands on the oversized apron she wore over her Sunday dress and went to hug him. "You are family. I'm not so sure I'm going to like Fred or this Ken that Tally is bringing home either. Dee says if they don't like me we'll drown them in the lake."

"What's not to like about you? You are perfect." Jack talked to Bodine but looked at Dee.

"Jack, you get the electric knife out and carve this ham," Roxie said. "It's a quarter 'til four, and I told them to be here on time. We're eating at four o'clock sharp and those who aren't here will have to eat cold, ungraced food."

"Yes, ma'am." Jack fished around under the cabinet and brought out the knife.

He wore pleated khaki slacks and a dark green shirt with a button-down collar. His hair feathered back from his face, and his eyes twinkled. Dee had to work to keep from staring at him like a besotted teenager.

Jack is the only one in this kitchen who looks normal. And for the first time in my life I love all of it, even the ones who are standing really close to the line dividing the rational from the insane.

Roxie had chosen her signature ruffles. Flowing orange silk pants with two-inch ruffles sewn into the side seams. Matching blouse with ruffles at the neckline and wrists. Pearls around her neck and in her ears. Orange Italian leather high-heeled pumps. Her red hair was fluffed up to brand new heights, and she wore blue eye shadow and extra blush.

Bodine had argued that she wanted to wear a pilgrim costume, but Roxie had put her foot down. The child could choose a Sunday dress, but it could not be white and she was not to wear white shoes. After all, it was long past Labor Day and that was the cutoff point for wearing white in Roxie's house. So Bodine was dressed in a deep burgundy velvet dress with a square neckline, a small ruby pendant in the shape of a B that Jack had given her for her birthday, and black patent-leather Mary Jane shoes.

Dee had chosen a slim, fall floral skirt that grazed her ankles, loden green suede boots, and the same color sweater. Roxie had sent Tally upstairs half an hour before to get dressed, telling her that jeans and a T-shirt would not do on the day she'd invited her professor to dinner. No sir, Tally would present a pretty picture or she and the professor, Ken, would dang sure be eating out in the yard.

The doorbell rang, and Tally yelled from the dining room that she'd get it.

"He's here," Bodine whispered.

"Take off your apron," Jack whispered back. "Go on out there and decide whether we feed him or drown him. If we're going to drown him, we'll do it before he eats. No use wasting good food."

She giggled and slung open the swinging kitchen door into the dining room. Dee stuck a foot in the door as it swung back and motioned for Jack.

"Is this legal?" His warm breath brushed across her neck and she shivered.

"Probably not but I want to hear." She put a finger to his lips, amazed anew at the tingles that came from touching him.

"Hello, are you Bodine?" A deep voice floated through the dining room and to their ears. "I'm Ken and I'm very glad to be here today. These are for you. I understand you like to fish. So do I, and I make my own lures, so I brought you a half a dozen. Thought maybe you'd like this one. I made it with orange feathers since it is Thanksgiving."

"Wow!" One word said it all. "Did you really make these all by yourself? Will you show me how? After dinner you reckon we could go to the lake and try them out?"

"Sure, I'll teach you to make lures and I brought my equipment just in case you asked. Do you think we could ask your mom to go too? Hey, I see you are wearing pink nail polish. Maybe you could loan me some for a lure or two. I've got silver and red but I sure hate to go in the store and buy pink. It's kind of embarrassing to take that color up to the counter."

Bodine giggled.

Dee shut the door. "He's a wise man."

"Well, Hell's bells, Dee. I would have brought you some lures today if that makes a man wise," Jack grinned.

"He's a good man. I had him investigated," Roxie said.

"Roxie!" Dee and Jack both said at the same time.

"Don't either of you Roxie me. I'm too old to raise another child, so if Tally was letting her hormones control her and this fellow was selling drugs to the students, or gambling away every dollar he made, I needed to know early on in the game. He's forty years old, stable as a judge, drinks socially only, has been a professor at Murray for fifteen years, and is well respected. He doesn't have Tally in his classes, so that's why they can date without problems with the school. He was married once. It lasted five years, and his wife didn't

look like Tally. She was short, dark-haired, and His-
panic. So he's not on the rebound and hooking up with
Tally because she reminds him of his dead wife. Now,
take that ham to the table, Jack. Start taking up the
beans and corn, Dee. Tally, you take the rolls out of the
oven and put them in the basket." Roxie never missed a
beat when Tally pushed her way into the kitchen. "Oh,
and you look much better, by the way. That burgundy
makes your eyes shine and your hair look even lighter.
If Ken doesn't fall for you today, he's either near-
sighted or dumb."

Mimosa and Fred appeared just as Jack carried the
perfectly browned turkey and set it in the middle of the
table. Hurried introductions were made. Roxie told
everyone where to sit and bowed her head. "Lord, I'm
grateful for this day and for everyone gathered around
our table. Grant us your blessin's and overlook our
bellyachin's. Amen."

"Amen," Bodine said. "Now let's eat. I'm starving.
But leave room for dessert. Roxie's got pumpkin pie,
pecan pie, banana nut cake, and she even made banana
pudding."

"Jack, would you do the honors with the turkey?"
Roxie asked.

"You sure, Roxie?"

"I'm sure. As excited as I am to have all these folks,
I'd let that knife slip and cut my finger for sure. Now
Fred, tell me, where are you two coming from today
and where are you headed to?" Roxie turned her atten-
tion to the silver-haired man sitting beside Mimosa. His

face was all angles and his nose sharp, his hazel eyes set in a bed or wrinkles.

"Left a load in Omaha and picked up one to take to Houston. This is one fantastic dinner. I can't remember the last time I set up to a table like this on Thanksgiving. Thank you for having me." He scooped up a double portion of cornbread dressing and topped it off with giblet gravy.

"How's it going, Mimosa?" Dee asked from across the table.

"Wonderful."

Dee believed her. She looked better than she had in years. Her hair had been stylishly cut into layers, frosted blond. She wore a tailored navy-blue pantsuit with gold buttons and navy pumps. Fred had forgone a tie but had on a white Western shirt with pearl snaps which was tailored to fit his tall, lanky frame, navy Western-cut dress slacks, and ostrich boots. They really looked like Bodine's grandparents.

"So you are Bodine? I brought you a prize out in the truck for after dinner," Fred said.

Bodine's eyes lit up.

Jack finished carving a portion of turkey for everyone and sat down at the other end of the table. Dee was on his left with Mimosa and Jack beside her, Bodine on his right, and Tally and then Ken on down the table. So the men were courting Bodine. At least they weren't stupid. If she liked them, they'd have stomachs full of turkey and not lungs full of water.

"I didn't even help pick out your prize." Mimosa looked across the table at her granddaughter.

"What is it, Mimosa?" Bodine eyed Fred from her peripheral vision. He looked like what she'd always thought a grandpa should look like and wondered if she should call him Fred or what.

"May I ask a question?" Ken said. "Why does everyone call everyone else by their name and not Mother or Grandma?"

Tally giggled. "Because . . . help me out here, everyone."

They all chimed in at the same time as if singing a hymn in church. "Because, only God and General Lee have titles. The rest of us have names."

"I see." Ken grinned.

He wasn't what a person would call handsome by any means. His face was round and rather babyish. He carried twenty extra pounds all in a roll around his waist, but his eyes were full of life and they softened whenever he looked at Tally or Bodine.

"So you'll be Ken forever in this house," Bodine told him. "Now pass me that cranberry sauce."

"Yes, ma'am." He nodded.

Dee ate slowly, listening to the conversation, watching everyone, afraid to blink for fear she would miss something. For the past seven years, Thanksgiving had been a formal business affair catered at the Suddeth home served at six thirty after half an hour of cocktails. She didn't even realize she'd missed the family fellowship until that moment, and suddenly she guarded each word and moment jealously.

"What are you daydreaming about?" Jack whispered in Dee's ear.

Mimosa was filling everyone in on her new husband. Fred had been married once, back when he was young, but the marriage hadn't endured a trucker's schedule. He had one son who was a career military man and was presently in Iraq, two grandchildren in Boston, and a lovely daughter-in-law.

"Just taking it all in. I love this," Dee answered his question simply.

"Missed it, did you?"

She nodded.

"Miss me?"

She patted his knee under the table.

"I'm not a puppy dog."

"I refuse to let you rile me today. It's too perfect. Don't Mimosa and Fred look happy? She's a changed woman. I think she's given up her hippie ways."

"I could make you mad in five minutes, but I'll let you have your perfect day," he said. "As far as Mimosa goes, don't put all the love beads in the attic just yet. It might be a phase."

After dinner Dee and Jack served coffee and dessert. Roxie kept the conversation flowing. Bodine wiggled and watched the clock. Darkness came early, and the adults just kept talking. She'd never get to use her new fishing lures if they didn't wind it down soon.

"Bodine, sit still," Roxie finally said. "It's too dark to be fishing tonight. You can take Ken first thing in the morning and stay all day if you want, but today is mine."

"But . . ." Bodine started to argue.

"What's the rule?" Tally pushed an errant strand of Bodine's hair back behind her ear.

"What you say is important and I have to listen to Dee and Mimosa, but Roxie is the queen and her word is the law," Bodine intoned in a monologue.

"That's right," Roxie said. "Ken is staying the night as well as Fred and Mimosa. This old bed and breakfast has rooms aplenty and there'll be lots of time for fishing tomorrow."

"Shucks," Jack muttered. "I thought I was going to steal Dee after cleanup. We were going to sneak off to the lake."

"Can I go?" Bodine piped up.

"No, you cannot. You've got a surprise from Fred in the truck and it'll keep you busy all evening," Mimosa said. "I'm finished with my pie, so I'll go fetch it so you can get your mind off the new lures."

"You two are on cleanup duty." Roxie looked down the table at Jack and Dee. "When you get finished, you can join us for lemonade on the back porch. The sun sets early these days. We'll have a bit of conversation, then you can go fishing."

"Too late after that," Jack said. "But we might go for a drive."

"That will be fine," Roxie gave her approval.

"What is it?" Bodine danced around when Mimosa came back into the room. "Did Fred really pick it all out? Oh, oh . . . look, Momma, it's that new computer game I've been wanting. How did you know? Oh, thank you," Bodine ran around the table to hug Fred tightly.

His face beamed. "My grandson is eleven and he loves this game. I figured if you were ever going to meet him that you'd better get good at it so he won't beat you too bad."

"He won't beat me," Bodine narrowed her eyes. "Can I go play it now, Roxie?"

"You don't want to join us for the sunset?"

"I'd rather play," Bodine said.

"Then you can play. No cussin'. No tears. No throwing the joystick when it doesn't suit you. Understood?"

"Yes, ma'am. When y'all adults get done, who wants to play with me?"

"Not me. That game gave me fits when I was making it. I'm sick of it," Jack said.

"You made that game?" Ken said.

"I did. It was the toughest one I ever designed," Jack admitted.

"I've been trying to get to level three of that game for a week," Ken said.

"Then you are brilliant. It's a tough one."

Tally slapped Ken's arm. "You've got to be kidding."

"No, I'm not. I'm addicted to that particular game and I'm not joking," he said seriously.

"You don't have to do this," Tally whispered when Bodine left the room.

"Have to! You're the one who's kidding. I've finally got someone to play against."

"I think I'm taking a back seat to my daughter," Tally said.

"Jealous?"

"As hell, but pleased as punch."

"Good, because I want to talk to you about something really important in the morning. Meet me on the porch, and we'll watch the sun come up all by ourselves. I'll bring the coffee and toast."

Jack moaned and patted his full stomach. He was slouched down in the corner of his sofa, his feet propped up on an oversized hassock. Dee had taken time to change into sweats before she followed him to the trailer. She'd taken off her Clifford the Big Red Dog house shoes at the door, fell onto the couch, and stretched her legs out until she shared the hassock with Jack.

"I'll have to pray extra hard tonight for forgiveness," he groaned.

"For gluttony?"

"That's right. Want to watch a ballgame?"

"Who's playing?"

"Cowboys."

"Then bring it on. Do you think they're playing on a full stomach?"

He flipped through the channels. "If they ate dinner, they're idiots. Well, dang it all, anyway, the game is over. I got my times all mixed up."

"Then bring on a movie. Not anything . . . ohhh, is that Patrick Swayze?"

"*Dirty Dancing,*" he said.

"That'll do. Haven't seen this one in years."

In fifteen minutes Jack had settled down into the cushions and was sleeping soundly. Near the end of the movie, Swayze's character was telling the leading lady that he'd never be sorry for what they'd shared that summer. That's when Dee began to cry. Not weeping or sobbing but silent, streaming tears.

I'm not sorry either. I'm going to let it go, let it go like that dust settling behind Swayze's old car. How could I be sorry for the past seven years when it brought me back to the place I am now? If I'd have stayed in Buckhorn Corner I could never appreciate what's here. It took that seven-year speed bump on life's highway to slow me down enough to make me see what I've got. Good Lord, what have I done? I love this sleeping man. Why have I been running from him?

The movie ended with an upbeat musical number. All the ends wrapped up neatly. The father wasn't so angry. The sister had come to terms with things. Swayze was still leaving, but there was hope that he might come back sometime in the future. When it ended, Jack awoke with a start.

"What'd I miss?"

"You'd be surprised."

"Who won? Cowboys or . . . who were they playing?"

"It was *Dirty Dancing*, and I think I won."

"Oh, yeah, it was a movie, not a game. Sorry I fell

asleep. Not very good company after a meal like that. Let's go raid the kitchen and have some more pecan pie."

Ray would have never raided the kitchen or let me watch an old movie while he slept on the sofa. But that's wrong ... I should not compare Jack with Ray ... but why not? Jack will come out on the positive end every time.

Dee held out her hand to pull him up from the sofa. "Let's go. I wonder how Roxie is doing with two men in the house."

"Don't I count?"

"No, you're family."

"Oh, yeah. Here we go with the brother thing again." He grumbled and refused to stand up.

She slapped him with a throw pillow. "I told you I'm not fighting today."

A cocky grin covered his face. He covered the space between them in one easy jump and wrapped her in his arms, tilted her head back, and lowered his head to kiss her. She wrapped both arms around his neck. Multicolored sparks swirled around them, sending them twirling in the middle of a high-powered kaleidoscope. She felt secure, happy, content, electrified, mushy inside. She wanted the kiss to go on forever. Pecan pie could wait.

"Tell me you didn't feel what I did," he breathed into her ear when the kiss ended.

"I don't know what you felt."

"Oh, yes you do. Now are we going to fight about that or are we going to go eat?"

"Eat if those are my two choices." She pushed him back and headed for the door.

"What other choice do you want?" He slipped his feet into his shoes.

"I'll tell you when I figure it out," she said and disappeared out the into the night, leaving him sitting there wondering what had changed while he was sleeping because something dang sure had. She'd kissed him back like she meant it and had hugged him tightly. What on earth had happened during that movie?

Chapter Thirteen

A cold, blustery north wind whipped across the full church parking lot. Women held their skirt tails down; men held their hats on. The few children who were there that Saturday afternoon were subdued. Skies were dressed in a solid sheet of gray, as if the earth was in mourning. Roxie wore ruffles but they were black, matching her shoes, veiled hat, and kid leather gloves. Her red hair had been subdued into a pristine bun at the nape of her neck. She entered the church and was ushered into the family waiting room.

Dee, Jack, Bodine, Tally, and Ken waited in line to sign their names to the guest list before being led to their reserved seats. Dee took a deep breath at the sight of the mauve-colored casket covered from one end to the other with roses: yellow, red, white, pink, coral, every color in the rainbow. She wondered where on earth the florist had found so many roses in the middle of December.

Soft organ music filled the church, but she tuned it out, instead going over a mental list of everything back at Roxie's B&B where the dinner after the funeral was planned for the family and Molly's closest friends. The church had provided lunch, but the evening meal would be much more private. Ham was already sliced and in the refrigerator. Baked beans bubbled in two crock pots. Plates were stacked on the end of the dining room table, cutlery arranged in a caddy. Dee stiffened slightly when she remembered what she'd forgotten.

"What?" Jack leaned over and whispered softly.

"Ice. We'll need more ice."

"I'll take care of it. There's lots over at the store."

The preacher appeared from a side door, stood quietly behind the lectern, and raised his arms. "Please stand for the family," he said.

Roxie led the way with Etta Cahill right beside her. They sat on the front pew together. Then Lucy, Molly's daughter-in-law, followed by the grandchildren and their families, Crystal, her husband and daughter, Katy; Maggie, her husband and daughter, Lauren; Hudson and his two sons, Jim and Bob; Stella, bringing up the rear with her father, Wes, his second wife, Sandy, and their daughter, Holly.

Etta's family sat across from Jack and the Hoopers, her son, Bob, his wife, Joann, and their two daughters, Jodie and Roseanna, all in a row. Dee leaned forward enough to see Roseanna. She glanced over and gave

Dee the hint of a smile. Her eyes were dull. Dee could see what Jodie had been talking about. Evidently, Ray had been right when he'd told her you could take the gutter out of the woman, but not the woman out of the gutter. Turn it around to say, you could take the woman away from the country but you couldn't take the country out of the woman. Roseanna wasn't happy.

"Please be seated." The preacher lowered his arms.

By the time the funeral was over and they'd made the trip across Sulphur to the cemetery, it had begun to sleet. Jack drew Dee close, keeping his arm around her for physical warmth as well as spiritual comfort. He knew what she was thinking without asking. The first of the great bed and breakfast queens had folded up her tent. Would Etta be next? Or Roxie? The thought of losing Roxie was enough to depress Jack; he couldn't imagine how Dee would handle it.

People scattered as soon as possible to their cars after the graveside service. Roxie joined her family in the van and led the way to Buckhorn Corner. She took off her hat, took off her gloves, removed hair pins, and fluffed up her hair, using a small compact mirror from her purse to check her makeup.

"We should have taken that trip last year, but Molly was in chemo and we couldn't. Now it's too late." Roxie dabbed black mascara from under her eyes and brushed powder across her red nose.

"Roxie, darlin', you and Molly and Etta took that trip every year. You didn't have to actually get on a cruise ship. You shared your lives, competed, laughed, cried . . . all of it, you did together. It was the same as taking the trip. Don't go whipping yourself at this point." Jack stopped at the stop sign just outside Chickasaw National Recreational Area and made a right-hand turn.

"You are right. How did you get to be so wise in such a short lifetime?"

"I had a good teacher. She lives right next door to me."

"Don't you go flattering me today. And can't you drive faster? We're going to be overrun in a few minutes and I want to have everything ready." Roxie's smile and eyes said she'd appreciated what he had said.

Etta, Molly, and Roxie—the three of them had shared their lives through almost fifty years. Molly was the first one with a bed and breakfast just outside the park, known then as Platt National Park. Brannon's Inn. She had made more beds and served up more meals than anyone in Murray County, Oklahoma. Roxie had bought her business next, and Etta followed suit the next year when she and her late husband built Cahill Lodge. They'd all three swapped recipes, told stories, looked forward to some vacationers and dreaded others. Now Molly was gone, leaving Roxie and Etta.

"Wonder what will happen to Brannon's Inn?" Tally said.

"She left it to Stella," Roxie said.

"Really? Not to her son or to be divided amongst all four grandchildren?" Dee asked.

"She told me last month she'd redone her will. She was of the opinion her son didn't deserve it. Those

Brannon men were worthless. Molly's husband ran off and left her when Wes was a little boy. She raised him in the inn, same as I did Mimosa. Then Wes married Lucy, had those three kids, bam, bam, bam, and started cheating on Lucy. She tried to save the marriage by having Stella, but it only worked for a little while. When Stella was a just a kid he left Lucy to marry his second wife, Sandy. They had Holly, who must be about eighteen now. Anyway, Molly left everything she had to Stella. Said she needed it worse than the rest of them."

"And she was hoping Stella would come home and run it, wasn't she?" Dee asked.

"Stella can't sell it for five years," Roxie said.

Jack turned into the driveway. The red house stood out like a beacon in the gray day.

"Why would she want to?" Bodine asked. "I wouldn't ever sell our house."

"You aren't going to grow up and marry a spoiled little boy who thinks he's pretty." Roxie patted her knee.

"Why five years?" Dee asked as they all made haste to get inside out of the cold freezing rain.

"Hopefully she'll come to her senses by that time." Roxie removed her coat just inside the door and handed it to Bodine. "Take all the coats back to the guest room. When the people arrive, you're in charge of coats."

"Yes, ma'am." Bodine didn't argue.

The house filled up quickly the next thirty minutes, people gathering around the table to fill their plates, finding a place to sit, moving from one group to the next when they were finished. Remembering the times Molly had filled their lives with adages, humor, scoldings; regretting the days when they hadn't come home often enough; not looking forward to the future without her.

Toward dark, Dee was sitting midway up on the staircase. Food trays were still half full. Ice and drinks weren't running low, so she watched the people in their little groups. Lucy, Wes, and Sandy were at least civil to one another. Dee wondered if she'd attended Ray's aunt's funeral if she and Angie would have been even that. Probably more like coldly formal. She was envisioning that scenario when Stella wedged in beside her.

"I don't know what's more difficult, losing her or trying to fill her shoes," she said.

"I'm so sorry." Dee patted her hand.

"We haven't done so well, have we Dee? Rosie's not happy up there in Tulsa, even though she's got the world by the tail. I'm miserable in California. Wondering from one day to the next if we're going to make rent. Mitch is so mad he could chew up railroad spikes because this property is tied up for five years. When Granny Molly died, his first reaction was 'How much do you get from the estate?' Tally does seem more content than I've seen her in years. Maybe we just have to get six or seven years older."

"Tally is engaged as of last week. This professor she met in Tishomingo. He's forty. Stable as they come. Loves Bodine. Roxie likes him."

"Wow! That says it all in three words . . . Roxie likes him. When's the wedding?"

"Right now the official date is June first. School will

be out. Bodine won't have to change schools in the middle of the year. He's planning a long trip for the three of them in his motor home as a honeymoon. Grand Canyon, the Redwood Forest, the beach somewhere around Pensacola, Florida, Disney World in Orlando, up to New York for the educational end of it with the Statue of Liberty and all that, then back through the north to see Mount Rushmore."

"Was he the one sitting beside her at the funeral?"

Dee nodded. "But to answer your question, no, we haven't done so well, but I'm learning not to be bitter. That broken road I chose at least circled around and brought me back home where I belong."

"What did you say?" Roseanna joined them, sitting a couple of steps down and looking up.

"I heard Rascal Flatts' lead singer singing a song about blessing the broken road that led him back home and suddenly it was clear that that's where I was in life. I've been down my own personal broken road and now I'm home. It's not easy blessing that road and all I had to travel through, though."

"Hmmmm," Roseanna pondered, the words of the song playing through her mind as she sat there.

"Your husband with you?" Dee asked.

"Oh, no, not Trey. Molly would have had to make an appointment to pass on at a certain time on a certain day six months in advance for Trey Fields to be here."

"I was surprised to hear you'd married someone from Tulsa. Last I heard there was a rumor you and Kyle Parsons would be tying the knot before long," Dee said.

"Would have but he got a stubborn streak one night and laid down the law about me singing in Jodie's place out at the Arbuckle Ballroom. Trey's limo broke down out on I-35 and he wound up coming in to call for help. Looking back, I wish the service station would have been open and he'd have never come inside the Ballroom."

"That bad, huh?" Stella asked.

"No, not really. He's a good man but . . ."

"Right," Dee nodded.

"It's those buts that get in the way isn't it?" Stella said.

"Granny Etta told me I wouldn't be happy without the smell of cows, dirt, and sweat around me. But I figured I was smarter than she is." Roseanna tried to giggle, but it almost came out a sob.

"Those queens are never wrong, are they?" Dee said.

"If they are, they hide their mistakes so well we'll never find them," Stella said.

"So what are you going to do with the inn?" Roseanna asked.

"I don't rightly know. I fly back to California tomorrow morning. There's about two thousand dollars left of the money she left that I can have right now. The rest is tied up in a fund only to be used to run the inn if I come home and do it. Mitch is so mad he won't even take my calls."

"I'm sorry this is so tough," Dee said.

Stella shrugged. "I made the bed. I guess I'll sleep in it. Let's talk about something happier. What's going on with you and Jack? Who'd have ever thought he'd be so darn good-looking when he was a teenager?"

"I'm not sure anything is going on with me and Jack," Dee said.

"Don't kid us. We aren't blind. That man has never let you get out of his sight all day," Roseanna said.

"You know, being the grandkids of the old queens, I figured we'd never lose contact," Dee said.

"Let's don't do it again," Stella said.

"No, let's don't. Molly would have liked for us to be sitting here on the steps like this," Dee said.

Stella wiped away a tear. "Think we'll ever be the queens of Murray County?"

"God, I hope not," Dee said. "I don't think I'll ever be wise enough to wear Roxie's crown. It's too big and important."

Later after everyone left, after Jack had dashed through the freezing rain to his trailer, she pulled back the drapes in her bedroom and watched the tree limbs bowing under the weight of the ice. Everything she saw or touched seemed symbolic and gave cause for profound meditation.

She thought about living to be more than eighty years with no one, the way Molly had. When Molly had thrown her husband out for his philandering ways and raised Wes alone, had there ever been a good friend in her life that she was terrified to trust?

The questions would never be answered, but she pondered them anyway. She loved Jack and the physical attraction was almost unbearable. When his fingers grazed her arm as he helped her out of her coat, jolts shot through her heart. When he looked at her with those intense eyes, she wanted to drag him off to a cave and never let him out of her sight. Being just his friend was so hard.

"Why do I have to be?" she said aloud.

"Be what?" Bodine asked right behind her.

"You are supposed to knock, lady," Dee said.

"I did, but you didn't answer. Tell me one more time that I'm not dreaming and I'm really going to have a father and his name is Ken. I'm afraid I'll do something wrong and ruin it." She wrapped her arms around Dee and hugged her close.

Dee hugged back. "You can't ruin it. Have you had a big fight with Ken yet?"

"Yep, he beat me at Monopoly and I got mad and he said I'd get over it, not to be a poor sport. That's the same thing Roxie says."

"Then he's wise like Roxie and you shouldn't get mad at him for that."

"Why are you standing here looking at Jack's trailer?" She changed the subject abruptly.

"I'm trying to figure out some things that aren't easy to figure out."

"Like whether you're going to marry him?"

"You've got marriage on the brain since Tally is so happy these days. You're probably thinking you'll get two pretty dresses if you get to be bridesmaid in two weddings, right?"

"Don't treat me like a two-year-old. I'll be in middle school next year."

"Things are simple when you are eleven," Dee said.

"Oh, yeah, well then I hope I never grow up. I'm going to my room to read. I love you, Dee."

"Thank you, Bodine. I love you too."

She shut the door softly and Dee went back to staring out the window. Soft yellow light flowed through his living room window out into the dreary evening, putting out warm rays across the freezing rain.

Symbolism again . . . warmth gushes from Jack and it wraps itself around my icy heart. Out of the mouths of babes! I have made a mountain out of a mole hill. I can trust Jack.

Suddenly she knew what she had to do or she'd spend another sleepless night tossing and turning. She just hoped it wasn't too late. Like Roxie always said, 'There's a time when it's too late to do what you should have been doing all along.' Dee held her breath as she slipped out the back door and jogged to the trailer.

When the cleanup was finished, Jack darted across the two lawns, flung open the door to his trailer, and rushed inside where it was warm. He and Ken had worked with the ladies putting leftovers away and picking up stray glasses to load into the dishwasher. If the weather kept up like this all night, he wouldn't open the store the next day. Winter, and especially December, was like that. Even the most religious fishermen, those who did their worshipping at the Wal-Mart store in front of Zebco rods and reels, didn't brave sleet in December.

He put his long black coat in the closet just off the living room, picked up the remote, and turned on the television to an old rerun of *Law and Order* before he went to his bedroom to change into sweats and a T-shirt. He carefully hung up his black three-piece suit, tossed the white shirt in the laundry basket, went through the day's mail he'd thrown on the dresser that morning, and put a CD of Mark Chesnutt into the player. The first song talked about a city girl and an old country boy. That was the way he'd thought about Dee. She was the city girl and he was just an old country boy. Some of the rest of the song didn't apply to them, but it seemed that everything he touched made him think of her. The song mentioned that the city girl hadn't been loved at all until old country came to town. In the depths of his heart, he didn't think Dee had been loved, not like he loved her. But did he love her enough to wait indefinitely for her to figure things out? Enough to give her that much space while he ached to hold her, to kiss her, to start a life with her?

"Yes, I do," he said and turned off the music. "Yes, I do. She's worth waiting on and fighting for."

When he came back out into the living room, Dee was curled up on the sofa.

It had taken every bit of nerve she could muster up to make herself walk across those two lawns to say her peace. She was terrified but it had to be done. Since

Thanksgiving she couldn't sleep, had no appetite, was edgy, and even Roxie had asked several times if she was coming down with the flu.

He sat on the far end of the sofa. "What's the matter, Delylah Loretta?"

"Why are you second-naming me? I didn't do anything wrong."

"Did you come over here to pick a fight?"

"No, I didn't. Actually the furthest thing from my mind was arguing with you, Jack. I've been thinking . . ."

He touched the scar on his face. "Oh, no! Don't tell me that. The first time you said that—"

"I remember. I didn't come over here to talk about it either."

"The next time you said you'd been thinking it was to tell me you were leaving with Ray. It left a different kind of scar."

"I'm sorry for both. Now, can I talk without you interrupting?"

"Only if you aren't thinking of going somewhere far away."

"Well, I was thinking of moving out of Roxie's house. It's plenty big but I've found something I like better. Something cozier and smaller."

Jack's heart turned into a solid chunk of ice and plummeted to the bottom of his soul. When had this happened? He'd thought they were making progress toward a lifetime together.

"Where? Please tell me you aren't going back east again."

"Actually, south."

"Florida?" He could sell the store and trailer.

"Closer."

He hated Dallas but if that's where she wanted to live he'd suck it up and manage. "Texas?"

She put her fingers across his mouth. "Shhhh. Let me talk. I prepared this big long speech and most of it has already flown out the window, but I've got to say the words so you'll understand. I figured out a lot on Thanksgiving and I've been fighting it for two weeks, but today when I looked at Molly in that casket I wondered why I was battling with my heart. It didn't lie to me all those years ago. It just let me have my way."

Jack frowned. What was Dee trying to tell him? That she was tired of Buckhorn Corner and ready to do something big and wonderful? Perhaps seeing Tally getting an education and so much in love had encouraged her to make the decision to go to college. Then she'd meet someone like Ken. A lump grew in his throat.

"Jack, I love you."

"Oh, no, please don't say that. Every time you do, you follow it up with something about loving me like I'm your brother or favorite cousin."

She scooted across the sofa and wrapped her arms around his neck, looked deep into those worried eyes and pulled his lips down for a kiss. "No, I really love you. I mean as in 'love you.' I'm here to ask you to marry me."

Jack was stunned into silence.

She leaned back to study his face. Maybe she should have only told him she was ready to date him, move in with him, something else other than proposing to him right there on the spot. But seeing Molly in that casket had reminded her that life was short and she had no guarantees of tomorrow. "Well?"

"Are you sure?"

"I've fought it ever since I came home, but these past two weeks have been horrible. I want you to hold me. I want to wake up in your arms. I want a yard full of kids and I want you to be their father. Jack, my heart is only half a heart without you."

"When?"

"Oh, I hadn't thought that far. Tonight?"

"How about tomorrow? We can go to Dallas, call Roxie from the hotel and tell her then? Or do you want to announce it in church tomorrow and have the traditional six-month engagement?"

"How about next Friday night right over at Roxie's house? That way it'll give her something to take her mind off Molly being gone. We'll only have the family. I'll call Mimosa and see if she and Fred can come. Ken and Tally, of course, and Bodine, and the preacher."

He groaned. "A whole week. That's eternity."

She kissed his eyelids and worked her way down to his lips. "It'll go by fast, I promise, and then we can go on a honeymoon."

He wondered if he'd fallen asleep and this was another one of the dreams that had haunted his nights so often the past six months. If it was, he danged sure didn't want to wake up. "Where do you want to go?"

"A faraway island with white sand on the beach and no people. The time will pass quickly. I don't know who I'm trying to convince. Me or you. We'll just have a simple wedding, and honey, I don't care if the honeymoon is right here in this trailer as long as you put a sign on the door that tells everyone to stay away."

"You'll have your island, Dee. I know just the place. One little cabin on a very private island with white sand on the beach. Have to charter a plane to get in and out of the place. I'll call tomorrow and take care of arrangements. How long of a honeymoon can we have?"

"A week. Then we'll be home for Christmas with Roxie and the family." She tilted her face up to his. "Kiss me again. God, I'm glad you never kissed me in high school. We'd have six kids by now if you had."

He leaned forward. "I love you and you can trust me."

"I know that, Jack. Down deep, where it counts, I know."

"Welcome home, Delylah Loretta."

"Glad to be here," she said just before the sparks began to fly.